Savaged Surrender

JENNIFER LYON

Savaged Surrender
Copyright © 2016 Jennifer Apodaca
All rights reserved.

Cover Design: Jaycee DeLorenzo of Sweet 'N Spicy Designs
Editor: Sashaknighteditor.com
Copy Editor: http://www.kimberlycannoneditor.com/
Formatted by: Author E.M.S.

Published by JenniferLyonBooks
www.jenniferlyonbooks.com

ISBN: 978-0-9967169-7-0

acknowledgments

I'm incredibly appreciative to so many people for their help on this book. First a shout out to Rebecca Zanetti for being the catalyst for this novella. I met Rebecca years ago at a writer's conference, and we became friends. Rebecca is hugely supportive and if you haven't read her books, I highly suggest you check her out. She's awesome!

Thank you to my friend and critique partner, Marianne Donley. There's a point where Marianne saves my butt on every single book by doing emergency reads and critiques for me. This book is no exception and I couldn't have written it without her help.

I need to say a heartfelt thank you to my editor, Sasha Knight. Sasha works tirelessly to shape my books into the best possible read while protecting the heart of the story. I love how she pushes me to develop the plot and characters to their fullest potential. Yet for all her amazing talent, she still can't break my Bad Comma Habits. I'm wild and reckless with those little guys.

A big thank you to my copy editor, Kimberly Cannon. You're my last line of defense in ferreting out mistakes and I'm so pleased to have your eagle eye go over the book.

Of course, all mistakes that get through are my own.

– Chapter 1 –

FOR A FEW HOURS ETHAN Hunt was living the dream by cooking in the kitchen of Stilts, the newest upscale restaurant that stretched out on pilings over the bay in San Diego, California. Surrounded by gleaming stainless-steel worktables, industrial stoves, wicked-sharp knives and the drone of voices yelling out directions, he got to work with the one thing he loved most in the world—food. All under the watchful eye of Chef Zane.

The frenetic yet focused energy in the kitchen was similar to being in the gym back when he'd trained to be a mixed martial arts fighter. That was before he'd fucked up so royally that he destroyed his reputation, his ability to fight professionally ever again, damn near ruined his health and earned a pile of debt as deep as the sea.

"How's this?" His assistant for the day held up a pan.

He glanced over and couldn't bite back his grin. Ana Kendall was a mess. Her dark-rimmed super-cool glasses were askew on her face, dark-blond hair scraped back into a ponytail, and her white apron was

1

covered in...hell, what was that? She must have spilled virtually every sauce in the kitchen on herself. Knowing her, she'd managed to taste all of them in the process. But she proudly held up the pan of crusty rolls he'd had her hollow out to toast for his goat cheese bruschetta.

"Perfect." He'd fix the uneven rolls when she got distracted by something else.

Chef Zane snorted behind them.

Ana shot him a look over her shoulder. "Still want that premium suite at Petco Park?"

The man's judgmental scowl morphed into a contrite expression. "Best work I've ever seen."

She nodded. "Thought so."

Ethan narrowed his eyes. "You offered him your dad's suite at Petco Park?" In trade for Ethan's chance to cook with Zane? Her dad had passed away suddenly less than two months ago. The shock and grief had rocked her, although in typical Ana fashion she was bouncing back quickly. But this? Her dad, a former professional baseball player, had prepaid for a suite at Petco Park baseball stadium for several of the Padres' home games. She was giving that away? "Ana—"

She cut him off with, "I need to change clothes."

Right, not the time to bring it up. Whatever she'd done to get Ethan this chance to cook with one of the best chefs in San Diego, he couldn't alter it now. Nor did he want to upset her in front of Zane and the staff by talking about her dad. He focused on her comment. "Why change? It's just us." He was cooking dinner for the two of them, and he didn't care if she wore shorts and a T-shirt. "Take your apron off and you'll be fine. Oh, and you might want to wash off the..." he reached up, rubbing his thumb over the smudge on her smooth cheek, "...soy sauce?"

Her brown eyes sparked, and a grin curved her mouth. "Chocolate. While you made the potatoes, Zane let me taste some desserts."

Figures. Ana's genuine friendliness and curiosity attracted people, and Zane was no different. Of course he wanted to show off his kitchen to the pretty girl. "You're supposed to be my assistant, little traitor."

God, he was going to miss her. Over the last few months, she'd become his closest friend. He could talk to her about anything. Well, almost anything; some subjects were off-limits. She didn't see the ugliness in him, and he wanted to keep it that way.

Ana sighed. "I'll make it up to you by eating the food you cook." Raising her eyebrows, she added, "Even if it tastes awful."

Her smart mouth amused the hell out of him. He leaned down, his face close to hers. "You'll eat it and love every mouthful." She always tasted every single dish he attempted. Ana was pretty fearless when it came to food and anything athletic.

Challenge gleamed in her eyes. "Or what?"

"No dessert."

Outrage yanked up her shoulders and puffed out her chest. "You can't do that. I have connections." She looked at Zane for help.

Ethan stepped in front of the man, cutting off her view. He easily had a foot in height and a hundred pounds on the little fireball. Not that he could intimidate her; she'd figured out quickly he'd never hurt her.

"I'm the chef tonight. I decide if you get dessert." Oh yeah, he loved taunting her.

"Is that right?" Ana's mouth quirked. "FYI, Chef Ego, I have frosted sugar cookies at home. I was going to be nice and send them with you to eat on your flight

3

tomorrow. But you continue irritating me, and I'm going to keep them for myself." She turned and flounced out, her hips twitching in her shorts.

Ethan yanked his gaze away from her ass. Nope, not looking. *Friends.* They were friends. Ana wasn't some chick he'd bang and never think about again.

"Damn, she's cute."

Ice slid into his veins at Zane's comment. The man had to be a decade older than Ethan's twenty-two years. "Get your eyes off her ass. She's too young for you. Still in college." He didn't care if Zane was the toast of San Diego's culinary culture and becoming a cooking celebrity, he wasn't good enough for Ana.

The man rolled his eyes in his signature dramatic fashion. "I wasn't the one staring at her ass."

A guilty flush steamed his skin and irritated his conscience. *Off limits. Ana is off limits.*

"Are you two dating?" Zane asked.

"We're friends. I'm leaving town tomorrow."

"Right, she mentioned that. But..." Zane's attention drifted to the door, and his brows drew together. "She went to a lot of trouble to make a special evening for the two of you. I don't normally allow anyone in here to cook other than my staff, but she swore you have some cooking skills and won't annoy the shit out of me."

An odd sensation raced down Ethan's spine. Ana had given him friendship when most people avoided him after the news exploded that the up-and-coming MMA fighter had had a heart attack from steroid use at twenty-one years old. Called him a cheater, an ungrateful thug, a loser, a dangerous jerk...

And he was all those things. Every one of them. But sweet and sassy Ana Kendall befriended him and stubbornly defended him.

4

She was his sunshine. He'd been in a pit of black despair before she'd decided they'd be friends. And tonight she'd given him an opportunity to experience what it'd be like to achieve his dream of becoming a chef someday.

Zane went on, "That girl believes in you, man. It's more than friendship for her."

"It's not like that between Ana and me." He and Ana had agreed they were just friends. Ethan left tomorrow to join the protection and security team for the rock band Savaged Illusions's yearlong world tour. He wasn't sure he'd ever come back.

Probably not. His notoriety here in San Diego was another stain on him.

"Zane, got a problem," one of the other cooks called out.

"Be right there." The chef shot a look at Ethan. "Never seen any girl go to so much trouble for a *friend*. Might want to make sure you're both on the same page before you leave tomorrow. Because that girl? Special." He stalked off.

Special. Exactly. That was the reason he refused to feel anything more for her. He wouldn't be able bear the look in her eyes if she found out about his past. Sure, she knew he'd been a runaway living on the streets. But she didn't know what he'd done to eat. The old shame slithered and mocked, the taunting female words echoing in his memory. *"Once a whore, always a whore."*

He squeezed his eyes shut and breathed to control the rage that had once driven him. He knew what he was—dirty. No decent woman would want him to touch her. Not in public, anyway. And most definitely not Ana. The girl was too damned good for him. He'd known it the second he'd seen her in Sugar Dancer

Bakery where she worked helping customers, taking extra time with the lonely older folks, making kids smile and just being Ana.

Then she'd turned all that sweet attention on him, and he'd been like everyone else who came into contact with Ana—helpless to resist her. So he'd compromised and walked the line. Friends. He wouldn't cross it.

They were fine. And tonight, he was cooking the best meal ever so they could enjoy their last night of companionship before he moved on to his new job. With renewed determination, he set about finishing the meal. He poured all his passion into the task, plating the crusted ahi and grilled sliced steak, potato and bacon au gratin, caramelized Brussels sprouts and the goat cheese bruschetta.

He took it all to a table against the glass wall of the open-air deck, surrounded by the bay glistening from the setting sun. It had to be perfect. His original idea was to bring Ana here for dinner, but she'd hijacked his plan, arranging for him to cook with Chef Zane. Now he wanted to give her the most delicious meal he'd ever prepared.

Something she'd remember when she thought of him, of their friendsh—

"Ethan."

Ah, there she was. After arranging the plates, he turned and froze.

Holy shit. Ana's hair fell in sultry waves around her face, and an electric-blue dress wrapped around her lithe curves. The hem ended midthigh, leaving too damned much of her tanned and toned legs bare, right down to her silver strappy heels.

His breath locked in his chest, and a buzzing filled his head. *Look away. Stop ogling her.*

But he couldn't stop. His control was taking a hell

of a beat down. It wasn't just the dress—Ana was hot no matter what she wore. Nope, what blew his restraint out of the water was that Ana had taken off her glasses.

Her black-framed spectacles shouted *good girl* to him, and were a visual reminder that she was smart, sexy and way out of his league.

Unable to help it, he demanded, "Where the hell are your glasses?"

Okay, that growling reaction wasn't exactly what Ana had hoped for. "I'm wearing my contacts." Zane had let her use his office and private bathroom to clean up and change. She'd meant to dazzle Ethan into yanking her out of the friend zone and into his arms.

He didn't appear dazzled. The light from the sinking sun caught the golden hues in Ethan's blond hair and highlighted the harsh lines of his strong cheekbones and rigid jaw. His blue eyes darkened as he glared at her. Backed up by powerful muscles packed into his six-foot-five frame, his stare alone was usually enough to stop huge men in their tracks.

But Ana wasn't a man, and she was damned tired of waiting for Ethan to pull his head out of his ass. He thought he was ignoring the attraction between them for her own good.

Screw that.

She wanted him to get on that plane in the morning and go do the job. How could she not support his goals? Of course she did. The same way he supported her goal to earn her degree and even teased her that one day she wouldn't just work for Sugar Dancer Bakery, but she'd be part owner with her boss and friend, Kat. He wasn't wrong. She'd make herself so indispensable to her boss, Kat would beg her to be a bigger part of the company. That was how Ana did everything, full-on and making herself too valuable to ignore.

But before he left, she wanted to show him he had a reason to come back—her. Once the band's world tour ended and Ana had her degree, they could give a relationship between them a chance.

"Why?"

His sharp question cut into her spinning thoughts. "Why what?"

Ethan regarded her for a beat, then grabbed a chair and pulled it out. "Sit."

Ana strolled over and settled into the seat. She carefully spread the napkin over her lap, aware of Ethan standing at her right shoulder.

Dropping his hand on the table by her filled plate, he leaned down, caging her in. "Why are you wearing contacts?" His gaze tracked over her bare throat and shoulders before his jaw tightened. "And that dress?"

She tilted her chin up. "To remind you I'm a grown woman." Oh look, he doubled down on his glare by adding a squint that made him appear even more lethal and totally terrifying. Or it would be if she didn't know for a fact that he'd never hurt her. She pulled out her perkiest smile. "Is it working?"

"This isn't a date." His jaw worked as he enunciated each word. "Just in case you're confused."

Heat rolled off him, along with the scent of food and pure, clean male. She loved Ethan's competitiveness, his fierce determination to pay off his debts and make his own way in the world. His quick humor and patience also appealed to her. But it was the slightly dangerous glint in his eyes that sparked erotic shivers in her belly, and a heated desire to challenge him. It was the sexualized version of the same drive that had her trying to beat him on their bikes and playing video games.

"Well then, since you picked me up and drove me here—" because Ethan was insanely protective and had insisted, going so far as to borrow a car since he'd sold his, "—should I get a ride home with someone else? I could ask Chef Zane." She worked some real evil into her grin. "Then we can be sure it's not a date."

His mouth twitched. "Smartass." He took his seat across from her, then poured some wine in their glasses.

"In a hot blue dress," she added, and sampled a small sip of her wine. She was still acquiring the taste, but she didn't think her beloved orange soda would really pair well with dinner. "You could be a little threatened that I might pick up another man."

Setting his glass down, he lowered his chin. "Try it and I'll toss your ass in the car and take you home. Now."

His words hung there, tempting the hell out of her. What was wrong with her tonight? But she knew—she couldn't bear the idea of losing Ethan. It just really hadn't hit home until the last few days that he was leaving. "That's kidnapping."

"And? Think there's a law I wouldn't break to make sure you're safe? Zane's a good chef, but that doesn't make him good enough for you, sunshine."

Her pulse skittered up, and flutters winged around her belly. Part of her wanted to surge up and run toward the kitchen just to test him on that. But since she wasn't two years old, she controlled the impulse and teased him instead. "However will I protect myself once you're gone? I'll be bored and probably date all kinds of nefarious bad boys." She broke off a small piece of bruschetta and popped it into her mouth. The warm bite of bread topped with bright tomatoes, spices and a crumble of goat cheese made her moan.

He reached for his water glass. "Have you lost your mind? You're not dating bad boys."

She fought a laugh at the ridiculous order and dug into her ahi. So good, it practically melted on her tongue. "You're right, maybe it's better to skip dating and just hook up."

Ethan choked on his drink and slapped the glass down. "Hell, I deserved that. I can't tell you who to date, I just..."

She leaned toward him, desperate to hear his answer. Did he feel that sick sting she did when she thought of him with other women? "What?"

His jaw tightened. "Let's talk about something else. How's your dinner?"

She wasn't giving up but let him change the subject for now. Focusing on the food, she enjoyed the flavors and textures but most of all, she swore she could taste Ethan's passion for cooking in each bite. "Amazing. I love it."

He set his fork down. "Thank you, Ana. I wanted to bring you here for dinner, but this..." He lifted his hand. "When you told me to come over early because you had a surprise, I never thought it'd be a chance to cook with a master chef."

Hot pleasure warmed her. She loved making him happy. "Today was fun for me too. Some of my best memories are of us cooking together."

"*Us* cooking?" He squeezed her hand.

"Watch it, dude. I've chopped a lot of onions for you. When you're famous someday, I could probably claim a percentage of your income."

He rubbed his thumb over her wrist. "My cooking

helped you study and will ultimately lead to your success. I could claim a percentage of your future income. And I saved your life when you were dying of strep throat."

"Oh, now I was dying?" God he made her laugh. Ethan had shown up at her house to check on her, didn't like how dog sick she was and hauled her to urgent care. "I was fine in a couple days." After antibiotics and a lot of sleep.

"Pretty sure the doctor said you only had minutes to live."

Ana rolled her eyes. He'd make a totally exaggerated boast like that, but whenever Ana brought up the day he'd helped rescue her boss from a madman with a knife, he shrugged it off.

"But heroics aside," Ethan said. "I'll never forget this chance to cook with Chef Zane. Or you."

Do it now. I have to tell him how I feel. Her heart thumped. "I can't ever forget you." All her practiced words fled as a knot of desperation lodged in her chest. But she didn't want to lose this moment, and forced herself to go on. "I—"

"I've brought dessert and coffee." A smiling server carried a tray over. "Key lime pie and molten chocolate cake."

Ana resisted the urge to snap at the woman for interrupting them. The server was doing her job. Besides, the thing that kept them from crossing the line to lovers was that Ethan believed her too good for him. Talking wasn't going to convince him otherwise.

She had to show him she had a bad side too. For that, Ana needed privacy.

An hour later, he parked the borrowed Mercedes in one of her guest spaces, and they headed inside her condo. She loved her little home, but right now it felt too small and tight, like her skin. Her nerves pulled taut.

"Cookies are on the counter if you're still hungry." She gestured to the pastry box and headed to the fridge. Snagging two cold bottles of water, she inhaled a breath of cool air. When she turned around, Ethan was right there, looming only feet from her. She heard the soft whoosh of the refrigerator automatically closing behind her.

"I don't want cookies." He dragged his hand through his hair, his shirt pulling against his chest. Finally he dropped his arm. "You're my hardest goodbye, Ana. I'm not sure I'd have made it through these last months without you. You're my one good thing."

As she stood there with a bottle of cold water in each hand, her throat swelled. For seven years, she had done everything she could to make her dad and stepmom proud and never regret all they'd done to get Ana out of a bad situation and have her come live with them. Since that day, she'd been the ultimate good girl, always in control. It was exhausting, but with Ethan, she'd been able to let go a little bit. Yet the times when Ethan had almost kissed her and stopped, Ana hadn't pushed. Nope, she'd been the good girl, letting the man decided.

Either she took the risk of showing him how much she desired him, or she lost him because she really was exactly what he thought—too good of a girl to take a risk.

Setting the waters down, she hopped up on the counter in the place she'd sat many times while Ethan cooked. "This isn't goodbye."

Ethan settled his hands on either side of her hips, caging her with the force of his sharp attention. "Then what is it?"

Her mouth dried, and blood pounded in her ears. All the muscles in Ethan's arms bunched and strained. Power, restraint and a vibrant hunger pulsed into the air around them. He hadn't even touched her and her body hummed. A bright and fiery need throbbed low in her belly, making her want to break his rigid control and free them both.

Swallowing, she lifted her hands to his face. "This." She kissed him.

Ethan sucked in a breath and went utterly still.

Oh God, what if he rejected her? What if he hated that she threw herself at him? *No, don't give up.* She feathered her lips over his, pouring her caring and longing into each touch. All the days, weeks and months of yearning for his kiss flooded her system.

Ethan's control shattered on a groan. He sank the fingers of one hand into her hair, and plunged his tongue into her mouth. His palm slid down her back, gripping her ass and pinning her in place.

Yes. Her blood raced, heating her entire body. Sexy chills skated over her skin, and everywhere he touched left a blazing trail. Driven by a fierce urgency, she thrust her tongue against his, the wet slide sparking a fierce hunger.

Or was it the way he held her trapped where he wanted her? Not recoiling at her aggressiveness, but meeting it with his own? Wanting to get closer, she wrapped her arms around his neck. Her nipples ached, warmth swamped her belly, and deep between her thighs, insistent need pulsed.

His palm on her ass dragged her forward, shoving her skirt up and pressing her center flush to the thick ridge of his cock trapped in his jeans. The hard pulse against her panties tore a moan from her throat. Ana gripped his shoulders, rubbing along his shaft, desperation pitching up too fast and brutal.

"I knew you'd be like this." He skated his lips down her throat. "One taste of you and I'd lose my fucking mind."

His words and the warm, wet trail of his mouth sent more shivers from her nipples to her clit. She tunneled her hands beneath his shirt to feel his fevered skin over granite muscles.

With a low growl, his fingers on her hip tightened as he rocked his length along her cleft. Every thrust pushed her higher and she could feel his cock growing thicker, longer and more demanding. A reserve that had ridden her for years melted away, leaving her free to go after what she wanted.

Getting a hold of his hair, she angled his head up to kiss him again. She tasted their shared dinner and Ethan, the deeply male flavor that made her crazed for more. "Touch me. I can't bear it."

He wrapped his hand around her hair, restraining her. His eyes burned like a blue flame as he scraped his fingers up her thigh. "You have no idea the ways I can make you scream in pleasure."

She tilted her hips up, desperate to find out. When he didn't move fast enough, she caught his thick wrist, pulling his hand where she craved it.

The rough glide of his fingers over her swollen bud sent shocks of pleasure arcing.

"Ethan." Her cry ripped out. This was everything she'd dreamed. The ache ramped up to unbearable. She couldn't survive without him doing that again, harder and longer. She rubbed against his hand, chasing that rising desire with a wantonness. Only with Ethan could she be this free and wild. "Please. No one makes me feel like you do."

He jerked back, eyes nearly feral, cheeks flushed. "Goddammit." Fury swelled his shoulders. He clenched and unclenched his fists.

Her hands fell to the granite, and her stomach plummeted, all her hope crashing down into a pile of twisted pain. "What did I do wrong?"

She hated the weakness, the tiny part of her still desperate to just be enough. A little voice in her head said, *What did you expect? You're a pathetic little attention seeker, begging for it. He didn't really want you. You just imagined it.*

Stop it. This wasn't the same thing. Needing reassurance, she forced herself to look at Ethan.

Ruthless determination and regret dug into his face, making him appear older and harder. "Nothing. I'm the one who doesn't do relationships. Ever. I fuck, leave and never think about the chick again. Go find yourself a man who's good enough. I'm not that guy."

He snatched his keys out of his pocket and strode to the door. Opening it, he looked back for a breath of time.

Then he left, closing the door and breaking her heart.

– Chapter 2 –

AS PART OF THE PROTECTION team surrounding the band Savaged Illusions, Ethan Hunt took the lead, walking in front. The group headed down the hallway of the concert venue to a private elevator.

"Did you see the packed house? The audience was sick! We were on fire!" Lynx, the drummer, high-fived the bassist, River.

"Hell yeah," River agreed.

Ethan tuned out their talk as the car shot up. When the elevator doors opened, he and Hank exited first, scanning the Skylight Lounge located at the very top of the concert venue. Floor-to-ceiling windows revealed the Tampa skyline lit up against the night. About fifty people, all with VIP passes, lounged in plush gray couches and chairs grouped around a sleek black bar draped in soft lavender lighting. Once they heard the elevator arrive, every eye turned to them.

Ethan focused on the lead bodyguard in the VIP section. At his nod that everyone in the upscale bar had been cleared, Ethan stepped aside.

Instant pandemonium erupted as the crowd surged toward the band. Cameras flashed, people laughed and yelled. He recognized two well-known actresses and a football player. A few familiar groupies, including the head of their fan club. Two men in suits and—

No way. Whipping his gaze back, he homed in on the small, pretty woman staring at him. His entire body vibrated with surprise.

Ana Kendall. The spitfire of a girl who'd haunted his dreams and invaded his days. No matter how many women he'd hooked up with or how far he traveled, she was there in his mind.

What the hell was she doing in Florida at a VIP afterparty for Savaged Illusions? He hadn't seen her in eleven months.

An uncertain smile wavered on her lips before fading.

For a second, everything around him was drowned out by a crash of memories and regrets. His muscles twitched with the urge to go to her, touch and tease her until she smiled and laughed the way she used to with him.

Ana looked away, breaking eye contact to talk to another person.

Ethan automatically took note of her two friends, Franci and Chelle, hovering by her.

Ana was here. He couldn't get his brain around that fact. But he didn't have time to dwell on it as the band headed straight for the bar. Snapping out of his shock, Ethan moved with them, taking up a stance at the edge of the bar to keep watch.

The others in security settled around the room at their assigned posts. With the band's fame skyrocketing, the security team took zero chances. After Ethan checked the position of all five members of the band, another man caught his attention. Young twenties; longish, dark hair; blue eyes; thin build in an expensive V-neck shirt; tight black pants and high-end suede sneakers all screamed money. But the way he stared at Justice set off Ethan's internal alarms.

If there was going to be trouble, this nervous kid would be it. He hovered at the edges of the crowd around the band, barely blinking, his eyes following Justice's every move.

Otherwise, everything appeared to be under control. The servers were all cleared and familiar with working VIP parties, and the guests were behaving. Ethan did another room scan, keeping his focus on the job.

Not on Ana in that pretty green dress, ordering a drink.

A current of awareness sizzled through him. Ana was watching him. Damn, she looked sweet and sexy. Her dress dipped between her small breasts, fit her waist and flared out around her thighs. He couldn't figure out why she was here. The need to talk to her formed an internal push. He ignored it to do his job and visually swept the room.

Unable to resist, he stole another look at Ana.

But she'd slipped away to talk to her friends.

A half hour later, his neck muscles were cramped from the effort of keeping his focus on his job, not Ana.

Justice lifted his hand in a signal to Ethan and headed to a private hallway. Damn it, the man knew to wait for him. Ethan strode after him, and noted the nervous kid following Justice. Getting between the possible trouble and the lead singer, he keyed the mic on his headset. "Hank, escorting Justice to bathroom. Possible shadow." He described the kid.

"See it. Stay with Justice. I'll find out what the shadow's up to."

"Right." He keyed off and said to Justice. "Go

straight into the private hallway." This wasn't the time to get waylaid by fans.

The lead singer glanced over his shoulder. "Trouble?"

"You had a shadow." Ethan shot a quick look back to see Hank had stopped the kid. A heated conversation broke out.

Justice nodded, used to security controlling his life. Even things like taking a piss became an ordeal. Ethan nodded to the security guard watching the hallway to keep fans and staff out.

Once in the hallway, Ethan went into the bathroom with Justice to make sure the room was clear then headed for the door to wait in the hall.

"Ethan," Justice said.

"Yeah?"

"Give me a few minutes."

He got it. Sometimes it was a phone call one of the band members wanted to make, or even just a few minutes of no one pulling at them. "No problem." Ethan stepped out to the hallway and stopped in surprise at the girl talking to the other security guard.

"This is a restricted area." Josh told her.

Unable to resist, he crossed to them. "What's going on?"

Ana shifted her gaze to him. "Ethan, I, uh, wanted to say hi. I know you're working so maybe later."

He couldn't let her walk away and touched Josh's shoulder. "It's okay, she's with me."

The other guard nodded and Ethan led her deeper into the hallway where he could keep an eye on the bathroom door and Ana. "I can't believe you're here. What brings you to Florida?"

"Vacation with Franci and Chelle. We're staying at the Tradewinds Resort in St. Pete's." She licked her lips and shifted uneasily. "You look well."

The dress pulled tight against her breasts, and damn it, he didn't want to notice that. Or think of that last night when Ana had kissed him and he'd lost his mind. Two more minutes and he'd have had her panties on the floor and been balls-deep inside her.

Answer her. "Thanks, you too." She looked so damned good he had to dig his fingers into his palms to keep from touching her, and remember he was on the job.

"Franci and Chelle surprised me with the tickets to the concert and the VIP passes. I almost didn't come."

Because of him and the way they'd last parted? "What changed your mind?"

A grin touched her lips. "Franci and Chelle went to a lot of trouble to get the tickets and VIP passes, and I didn't want to ruin that for them."

How could he feel that pinch of disappointment when he was the one who'd pushed her away? What did he want, for Ana to have been sad all these months? God he was a selfish bastard. "How are you, Ana? The way I left—"

"I'm fine," she cut him off. "I graduated, and Kat promoted me at the bakery to the publicity director."

She seemed tenser, edgier than he remembered. Was it unease from seeing him again and the awkwardness stretching between them? Or something else? But the part about her finishing her degree and getting a promotion pulled a smile from him.

"Congratulations. You're a college graduate." While all he had was he GED, a certificate from culinary school, and his colossal failure as an MMA fighter. "I'm proud of you, sunshine." His old nickname for her slipped out before he could think better of it.

"Thanks. I'd love to hear about how you're doing." She swallowed and blurted out, "I was hoping if you have time, we could grab some coffee or lunch? I'm here all week. I don't know how long you're staying."

She wanted to meet? Before he could formulate an answer, his earpiece crackled. "Ethan, threat has been neutralized. Stay with Justice until he's back in view."

So either Hank had determined the boy wasn't a threat or had removed him altogether. Ethan touched the mic and answered, "Got it." He gestured to his headset. "Sorry, work."

"Right, you're busy. Well, you know my cell number, if you're around. Nice seeing you." She started to turn.

Unable to help it, he touched her shoulder. Her soft, warm skin beneath his palm sent a zap of heat straight to his dick. Memories pressed in and woke up the ache in his chest. Damn it, he'd missed her.

"Ana, wait." He dropped his hand.

Her shoulders tensed, but she faced him.

He didn't know what to say. Did he want to see her? Hell yeah.

But should he? "I'm here all week too. The band's taking a break after the show tomorrow night."

"Really?"

The spark of hope in her gaze made him pause. "Yes." He wanted to see her, but that last night in San Diego had made it clear—their attraction was so damned strong that with enough time together, they'd end up in bed. "But nothing's changed with me. I'm still not a relationship guy."

A flush crawled up her throat as she rocked on her heels. "I got that eleven months ago, loud and clear."

He'd embarrassed her. What was it about her that made him stupid?

"But things have changed with me."

Her words punched right into his chest and brought out his protectiveness. Changed, how? Ana didn't need to alter anything about herself. She was sweet, caring, ambitious and funny as hell. Why would she change? "What do you mean?"

She lifted her shoulders, every line of her small frame vibrating with resolution. "I grew up. I've been working hard to be what everyone else needs me to be. And that's okay, that's what I do. But right now, this is my vacation, and for a week, I'm looking for a chance to let loose and be a little bad with no strings attached."

Stunned, he struggled to think. "You want to be bad." With him? Jesus. No strings attached? Was this a prank? Or was this some kind of revenge? "Are you propositioning me?"

She compressed her lips. "God I suck at this."

He'd feel sorry for her if he had any idea what was actually going on. "At what?"

Sighing, she fiddled with the small purse hanging from her shoulder. "I wanted to meet and catch up, and if we still have an attraction, then yeah, I guess I'm propositioning you. But this time I'm not looking for anything more than a sexy fling and we go our separate ways."

He couldn't formulate an answer. Thankfully Justice was still in the bathroom, and no other band members had come into the hallway. "I don't know what to say."

"Right, okay." She forced a small smile. "If you decide you're interested, let me know." She turned and walked out of the hallway.

Did that just happen? With Ana? He got propositioned by groupies all the time. Sometimes he indulged and forgot them.

But Ana?

His muscles twitched with the need to go after her,

drag her someplace private and find out what the hell she was thinking. But he couldn't; he had to stay outside the bathroom door and wait.

Frustration screamed in his brain, and hot need pulsed in his gut.

What was he going to do?

Ana could feel Ethan's scrutiny searing her spine as she walked away. *Don't look back.* Her heart pounded from seeing him and the way she'd mangled that conversation. What was wrong with her, just blurting things out like that? She'd thought she'd been prepared to see him. But when all six feet five inches of him stepped off that elevator, it had been a punch straight to her heart. She'd missed him so much.

But she meant what she'd told Ethan, she'd grown up. She'd been out of line that night by trying to naively pull her friend into a relationship he didn't want.

Yet Ana had kissed him.

That humiliation still stung. And the way they parted—him walking out in anger and disgust was an ache that wouldn't quite heal. What if they could do it over? Recapture some of their friendship and all of that sizzling attraction? But this time Ana wouldn't push for a lasting romantic relationship. Instead, Ana and Ethan would both walk away with good memories. All she had to do was convince Ethan that she truly was ready to be bad while on vacation. But she'd handled that reunion with him almost as terribly as she'd handled that last night in San Diego. Clumsy and coming on too strong.

Franci approached her as soon as she got a few feet from the hallway. "Did you talk to him?"

"Yep." She'd rarely seen Ethan so shocked. Or maybe he'd just been struggling with how to turn her down.

"Well? Did you guys make plans? The band is on a break after tomorrow's show and staying in Florida for a week. It says so on their website."

"Stalker," she teased. Both Franci and Chelle had gone to a lot of trouble for tonight. Planning this trip to coincide with Ethan's schedule, buying the tickets and securing the passes to this afterparty. Their plot was a bit insane, but their hearts were in the right place.

"Hijacker. We had the perfect plan to help you. But no, you stole it."

Amused, she said, "I'm a hijacker?"

Franci nodded, her brown eyes full of alcohol-fueled sincerity. "You illegally seized control of our plan, which is hijacking. And you stole the keys to the rental car out of my purse. So you hijacked the plan and stole my keys."

Unable to help it, she tilted her head and said, "Are you sure I didn't illegally seize control of the rental vehicle, thereby hijacking it too?"

Franci chewed her lip. "The argument could be made... Hey. You're distracting me."

"'Cause I'm beautiful?" She was probably going to hell for toying with her somewhat inebriated friend. It was only fair since Ana had assumed the role of designated driver by swiping the car keys. Everyone knew the DD got teasing privileges.

"Funny. Our plan would have worked if you weren't a control freak who had to butt in and take over."

Ana laughed, even if there was an uncomfortable grain of truth in that statement. "Or maybe I came up with a better plan of being honest."

Franci raised her eyebrows. "Okay, so you took over. How'd that work out for you?"

Ana forced a brilliant smile. "Great. He's going to call me." Maybe. Okay probably not. Heading for the bar, she added, "Come on, let's have some fun." She'd tried, and Ethan would either call or he wouldn't. Either way, she'd handle it and be fine.

Franci joined her, ordered a vodka and cranberry, and then shot her a smug look. "Bet you're regretting your hijacking ways now. If you'd stuck to the plan, I'd be the DD."

Ana ordered an orange soda. "I'll be glad when I don't have a hangover tomorrow."

While they waited for their drinks, she watched as Ethan returned and took up the same post at the end of the bar she'd seen him at earlier. He stood with his legs spread, arms crossed and giving off an alert-and-ready-for-any-trouble vibe. She couldn't tear her attention from him. In eleven months, she'd never tried to contact him—not even in her most terrified moments. Oh she'd thought about it, and in a strange way that comforted her. Telling herself that if she truly needed him, he would come.

She wouldn't ever have called though. It was only a fantasy to get her through the nights of worrying.

Now she just wanted a chance to break out and, well, be bad. Safely. For so long, she'd done everything right, struggled to be perfect.

Would Ethan be interested? Could he see her as more than that college girl he'd known?

His gaze slid to hers, and her stomach flipped at the sheer intensity.

"Do you know Ethan?"

The voice startled her. Ana forced herself to turn to a woman with long blond hair flowing around her sculpted face and memorable brown eyes. "You look familiar... Oh! You're Chef Siena Draco." Ana loved her show on the Food Network.

"Guilty. I noticed you talking to Ethan earlier. So you know him?"

It seemed odd that anyone paid attention. Curious, she said, "He's an old friend. Do you know him?" What if they were lovers? She hadn't asked Ethan if he was involved with someone. The thought hurt way more than it should.

"Yep, we met at one of my restaurants."

"Wow." A celebrity chef was familiar with Ethan?

"Ana!" Chelle caught her arm, her blue eyes dancing with excitement. "Come meet the band. I just talked to them, they're awesome. I told them you know Ethan, and they want to hear all about it."

Siena laughed. "Apparently, I'm not the only nosey one."

As she was swept away, Ana looked back at Ethan.

He was watching them, his mouth flat. She could almost feel the heat of his gaze sizzle over her skin. *Possessive*. Her stomach fluttered again. Was it just his old protectiveness? Or was the attraction still there between them?

Would he call her?

It'd been an hour since Ana's bombshell proposition that left Ethan buzzing with conflict and struggling to stay focused on his job. And lust, but that wasn't a surprise. He'd been attracted to her since the first time he'd seen her.

It was that good-girl thing.

And tonight? She'd just upped that to girl good wants to be bad. With him.

Seeing his boss striding toward him, he asked, "What's up?"

"Everything's quiet. A few people getting shitfaced, but no trouble. Go take a break before the band leaves. I'll cover your post."

Hank was a stickler for security getting a chance to stretch their legs, grab something to eat and let down their hypervigilance for a few minutes. Normally Ethan would snag a water and go outside.

But tonight, he had another goal and headed straight for the woman dominating his thoughts. Weaving through people clawing for the band's attention, he wrapped his hand around Ana's arm. "I'm on break, can we talk?"

She turned, her eyes wide. "Uh, sure."

He led Ana across the room to a high table tucked in a corner by the floor-to-ceiling windows. Holding her chair, he tried to ignore the enticing way her dress slid up her thigh. Why did he remember exactly what her skin felt like, and her shivers as he kissed her, his fingers trailing higher on her leg? The way she'd gotten demanding, needy, triggering a fierce urge to give her everything she wanted.

"You can say whatever you wanted to tell me," Ana said. "If you're not interested in seeing me, I'll accept that."

He clenched his jaw at the uncertainty swimming in her brown eyes. What had it cost her to come here tonight, face him and make the proposition of a no-strings-attached fling?

"I think about that kiss," he admitted.

Her mouth parted, and her tongue darted out to touch the tip to her plump bottom lip. "You do?"

"Yes. And I think about you." He ran a hand over his head. Did she have to look so damned beautiful

27

and sleek? By most standards, Ana was cute, with her heart-shaped face and tiny stature. But to him, she was gorgeous and untouchable. "But the reality is, I'm still bad for you."

Her chin notched up. "Bad is what I'm searching for right now. Short-term bad."

Heat blazed over his skin at the idea of Ana, his sweet girl, wanting to be bad. "Why?"

"I'm tired of being good, of always trying so hard, and worrying that I'm falling short. I'm ready for some fun, but I don't..." She looked away.

She'd been honest with him right up until now, so why was this hard? Or did she fear him rejecting and hurting her again? Catching her chin, he turned her face to see her expression. "Don't what?"

Her eyes shimmered with a need that nearly undid him. "I can't seem to find the guy I want to be bad with. Except for you."

Hell. He stroked his thumb along her cheek. "Ana. You don't even know what you do to me." He'd struggled every damned day they'd spent together battling their growing attraction. Now she was offering herself to him, with no strings and no guilt. How could he resist that?

Tugging his hand away, he searched for a distraction before his control could snap and he kissed her.

Not here. Not now.

He focused on her empty glass. "Can I get you something from the bar?" That would give him a minute to get his head on right.

She wrinkled her nose. "Nope. I'm DD tonight, so just sticking to orange soda or water, and I've had my fill of both." Shifting her attention on a point past him, she waved at a group. "They keep toasting me with their shots."

He followed her gesture to see Franci and Chelle laughing around Lynx, River and their entourage of the usual party chicks. They raised their glasses of whatever they were chasing the shots with, and made kissing faces at him and Ana.

"How did you end up DD, and why are they taunting you if it lets them have fun?" The Ana he remembered didn't drink much, especially for a college-aged girl, but he was curious.

"I foiled one of their insane plots." She shrugged. "This is their payback. But we'll see who's laughing in the morning. I'm so setting my phone to blast music at six a.m."

A chuckle rumbled up his chest at her gleeful voice. "I'll have one of the limos drive you back to the resort if you want a drink."

Surprise registered on her face. "You can do that? What about our rental car?"

"We have extra limos on hand tonight, it's not a big deal." He'd check, but if it wasn't being used, his boss Hank and the guys in the band wouldn't care. There were perks to the job. "I'll drive your rental to the manor where we're staying and bring it to you at the resort tomorrow." Ethan usually rode in the limo with the guys, but someone else could do it tonight.

"All the way to St. Pete's? It's a half hour to forty minutes from here."

Ethan leaned his arm on the table, enjoying being this close to her. "It'll give us a chance to catch up with each other. And talk about you wanting to be bad. With me."

"You're interested?"

He couldn't lie to himself or her. "I walked away once, and it only made me hungrier for you. But there's no future, Ana, not for you and me. That will never change."

"I know."

Her simple acceptance nagged at him. Why did she want this? Fast and hard sex and nothing more? For him, it was all he knew. But Ana...shouldn't she look for a real relationship? He started to ask her if everything was okay, but stopped himself. Once she'd have trusted him enough to tell him if something more was going on.

But now? After he'd left so abruptly that night, and then hadn't talked to her in nearly a year?

Yeah, time to ease up and give them both a little space. Instead he asked, "Want that drink now?"

"I think... Oh hell." Ana shoved off the high barstool.

Ethan shot up, automatically on alert. "What?" But he instantly saw the problem. Franci and Chelle were stripping off their tops.

Ana rushed over, pushing through the people gathering around. "Hey! Stop it!" She grabbed Franci's shirt, which was tangled around her neck, and forced it back down.

Ethan quickly caught the edges of Chelle's opened shirt and began rebuttoning it.

"No. We're shashing clothes."

He squinted, trying to make out the slurred words. "What?"

Furious, Chelle twisted in his hold, damn near ripping her shirt. "Ex-shash-ing."

It took him a second to work it out "Exchanging? Like trading clothes?"

"Yes! What I said."

"No," Ana said. "You can't exchange clothes with Franci."

30

"But we have a plan." Chelle stuck her bottom lip out.

Ana glared at him. "Don't you dare laugh."

"Too late." He couldn't help it. He saw this shit all the time. Ordinarily it was annoying, but Franci and Chelle weren't doing the usual dancing naked, swimming naked, trying to get screwed naked, or his least favorite, the dramatic female meltdown or temper tantrum. These two were original—they wanted to change outfits. Ana's friends were funny drunk or sober.

"Need a hand?" Hank asked Ethan, while two more security guards urged people away from the scene.

"I'm sorry," Ana said. "We'll leave. I didn't realize they'd had so much to drink."

Ethan stopped laughing at Ana's obvious distress. "Hey, no one's mad. They didn't hurt anything."

She nodded. "I'll get them back to the resort. Thanks for helping."

He caught her arm. "Take a limo. You can't handle them both while driving the car, and the driver can help you get them in the room." Chances were good the girls were going to pass out in the limo at some point.

Gratefulness filled her eyes. "Are you sure it's okay?"

Hank cut in. "It's perfectly okay, and Ethan's right. It's better you're not trying to drive and handle double trouble here." A smile twitched the man's mouth. "And don't look so distressed. These two were having fun. I've been watching them since they began doing shots. They had some plan for a fashion show..." He gave in and laughed.

Ana flushed again. "Thank you, uh..."

"Hank."

She straightened, obviously regaining her poise. "Hank. I'm Ana, and I appreciate your understanding."

He smiled at her, then said, "Ethan, help Ana get her friends packed up and on the road. Use Barb's limo. She can manage any problems."

"Limo!" Franci shouted.

Ethan nodded at his boss. "Got it." Together, he and Ana herded the girls down to the car. After coaxing them inside, he took Ana's arm. It was early morning, around one a.m., and the moonlight cascaded over her. "Text me when you're safely in the room and the details to bring the car back tomorrow."

"We'll be fine tonight, but I'll text you."

God he wanted to pull her against him and kiss her. But he was still on the job, and past experience warned him that a kiss with her could get out of control in seconds. "Ana."

"What?"

"Let me take you to lunch tomorrow. We'll talk and catch up, then if it's really what you want, we can move on to discussing the ways you can be bad."

Her eyes glinted with something. Curiosity? Mischief? "We can eat at the resort." She leaned toward him when noise from inside the car cut into the moment.

Franci and Chelle pressed their lips to the window, making exaggerated kissing gestures. Ana sighed. "It's going to be a long drive. They apparently aren't too drunk to remember Operation Kiss 2.0."

"Say what?" She'd lost him with that comment.

Ana caught his expression and laughed. "That's the name for their insane plot I mentioned earlier. They got the tickets to the concert and party, then planned to sneak off and leave me here so you'd have to take me back to the resort."

"They'd do that?" The idea of Ana stranded infuriated him. "That's dangerous as hell."

"They were going to tell you on their way out they had an emergency and ask you to get me back to the resort. They thought if we spent time together, we'd recreate the kiss of our last night together in San Diego."

She couldn't be serious. "The one where I walked out on you?" Ana and her friends teased each other, made hysterical bets with one another, but they'd rip apart anyone who dared to hurt one of them.

Ana's face flushed. "They don't know that part. I told them it was a hot kiss but we both decided the timing wasn't right since you were leaving."

"Why?" He didn't get it.

"Because they would have tried to find a way to get revenge on you if they thought you'd hurt me. This was simpler, better. Except now the tour will be over in a month and they assume you're coming back to San Diego."

Ethan glanced over at the two drunks now licking the window in a distorted parody of French kissing. Her meaning sank in. "Oh shit. They're matchmaking."

Ana nodded. "Yep. But it's fine. If we do have a fling, I'll tell them it just fizzled out. And if we don't, I'll tell them the chemistry died. See? Easy." Banging on the window had her sighing again. "I'd better get them back to the hotel."

Pulling open the door, he held it while she shooed Franci and Chelle back and climbed in. Ethan closed it and stepped aside as the limo slid away.

Why did he think letting her go a second time was going to be anything but easy?

– Chapter 3 –

"YOU GUYS GOING TO BE okay?" Ana snagged a bottle of Gatorade from the fridge in the kitchenette of their fourth-floor suite. The sun streamed in through the opened slider, along with the sound of the beach just steps away.

"Are you laughing?" Franci demanded. Both of them were sprawled on the couch, dressed in shorts and T-shirts, still looking pale with dark circles under their eyes.

"Not since six a.m." Ana held up her hand. "Swear."

"Bitch," Chelle snarled. "That was evil."

She poured the drink into two glasses. "It was funny as hell." She really had set her cellphone for one of Savaged Illusions hard rock songs. It blared out at the stroke of six. The girls had begged her to make it stop. "I can show you, I videoed it." She handed each of them a glass of the sports drink.

Franci shot her a glare. "I have footage on my phone from your birthday."

Okay, that was low. One look at that recording of her attempting to sing at a karaoke bar had cured her dream of stardom. "Fine. Truce?"

"For now," Franci agreed. "But you owe us. Our plan worked. Operation Kiss 2.0 was a masterful plan. Right, Chelle?"

"Hell yeah." She dropped her head to the back of the couch. "God I am never looking at tequila again."

Ana had coaxed them into drinking some water and Gatorade in the limo, and dosed them with Advil too. Overall she didn't think their hangover was that bad. They'd be raising hell in a few hours. "Wrong. I'm seeing him because I hijacked your plot and did the cleverest thing of all by asking him if he wanted to get together and catch up."

Chelle got up and crossed the room to touch Ana's shoulder. "We're trying to help you. We weren't there for you when you found that lump. You went through a lot in the last weeks, and..." She looked away, her eyes wide with regret.

"I'm fine. I've told you guys that. I showed you the lab report."

Crossing her arms, Chelle pointed out, "You didn't show me, I found it in your bedroom. We wouldn't have even known you had a biopsy."

Ana took a breath, hating the cold loneliness that made her feel like the outsider. She'd tried to tell them, but Ana didn't get to have problems. She had to be perfect, the girl who solved everyone else's crises. *That's not fair, and you know it. People can't help if they don't know.*

She fought down her misplaced anger and tried to soothe Chelle with, "I would have told you guys if they found something. There's no cancer, I'm fine. And damned lucky." Too many people in the world got the bad news. Ana had been very fortunate and had no right to the little pity party trying to suck her in. She was on vacation to celebrate her good health.

Chelle softened a bit. "I just feel awful. I know you tried to tell me, and I was so panicked over work and—"

A knock on the door cut her off.

"Chelle, stop." She and Franci had been alternating between guilt and anger at Ana for not making them listen. "It's over, okay?" She didn't want to dwell on it. "That's probably Ethan now." She narrowed her eyes. "Be good, and don't bring up the biopsy." Ethan wasn't there to listen to her problems. This was for fun, nothing else. She wanted to feel like a desirable woman and push her boundaries a little bit.

She went to the door and opened it.

"Hey." Ethan took off his sunglasses and did a slow study of her print silk shift dress in island colors, legs bare all the way down to her flats. "Now that was worth the drive."

A flush warmed her against the room's air-conditioning. She looped her purse over her shoulder and called out, "We're leaving."

Franci rushed up to them. "Hi, Ethan. Thanks for saving Ana from us last night."

"No problem." He tossed her the keys. "Here's the car back."

Franci caught them, then frowned. "How are you returning to your hotel?"

Oh crap. Ana hadn't even thought of that. "I could drive you."

He waved it off. "I had a rental car meet me here. I'm good. Come on, let's get something to eat." He held out his hand.

Franci bumped her from behind. "Two words," she whispered. "Vacation sex. Chelle and I are going shopping. You can have the room all to yourself."

One look at the grin on Ethan's face told Ana he'd heard. She put her hand in his and hurried out the door. It was either that or slam the door so she didn't have to face his teasing.

Ethan squeezed her hand. "It seems Operation Kiss 2.0 has been upgraded."

Once inside the elevator, she went for bluntness. "Despite Franci and Chelle's shenanigans, you're perfectly safe with me. If you decide this isn't what you want, we'll both walk away."

He stepped into her space, raising their joined hands over her head. "What if it's you who's not safe with me?"

Her breath caught as Ethan loomed above her in the glass elevator. There was nothing threatening in him though, it was...protective. "In what way? You'd never hurt me."

"I walked away eleven months ago because you were still in college, your father had passed weeks before that, and you were too damned vulnerable. But my restraint just ran out. Understand that once our time here in Florida is over, I will leave again. Don't mistake me for a good guy. We both know I'm not. So the question is, can you handle that?"

The elevator lurched slightly as it stopped. Ana stood perfectly still, relishing in the feel of Ethan's hand bracing hers against the elevator glass, and his eyes eating her up. Could she handle it? Damn right she could. It might hurt—okay it *would* hurt—but she understood that she wasn't going to come first with Ethan. He'd made that clear.

Tilting her head back, she arched a brow. "Now that you've done your grand speech, can we have lunch?"

The edges of his eyes crinkled. "You always were impatient to eat." He tugged her out of the elevator. "You have someplace in mind?"

Regaining her wits after that display of caveman

sexiness, she answered, "I'm taking you to the Flying Bridge. It's a dock out over the Gulf. It's too pretty a day to stay inside."

People wandered around in bathing suit cover-ups, shorts and sundresses, a few playing miniature gulf, splashing in the pool, some kids chasing each other and laughing. Once they got their seat on the dock and ordered, she let her curiosity surface. "Do you like doing security for the band?"

"I'm good at it. We've had some crazy stuff. Stalkers, psychos, one guy starting fires, and the women." He rolled his eyes. "I'd rather deal with a knife-wielding crazed man than a woman bent on trapping a rock star. They are devious little shits. The stunts they've pulled are insane."

"Wait, have you dealt with a knife-wielding crazy?"

"It's rare." He paused while the server set down Ana's Mediterranean vegetable wrap and Ethan's Philly special. After topping off their drinks, she left. Ethan took a bite. "This is good."

Worry for Ethan blared in her head. "But there have been knife attacks?" She knew his job had a dangerous element to it, but she hadn't dwelled on it.

"Had a guy with a knife go after Gray. We were hanging out in a hotel bar, but it was over in seconds. I saw the guy before he got close, shoved Gray down into a booth and disarmed the attacker. No one was hurt." He flashed a grin. "Okay, that's a lie. I caught Gray by surprise, and he smacked his face on the table. Had a bloody nose. Dude was pissed about that."

Oh God. "You weren't hurt?"

He gave her a look. "One guy with a knife, Ana. I saw him coming. If I'd been hurt, I'd have deserved it."

"I know." Ethan was capable and strong. He'd worked hard to shift his MMA experience into becoming the best security possible, including intensive weapons training. She was confident in his skills, but he was still her Ethan, and she couldn't help worrying. To distract herself, she picked up her wrap and took a bite.

Ethan stole one of her fries. "Stop fretting. The guy wasn't trained, just a nut. He believed that every time Gray chose to play the piano instead of keyboard, he was summoning the devil. Which is pretty funny because of the five of them, Gray's the most civilized."

"Civilized how?"

"He usually doesn't get into fights, trash hotel rooms, leave groupies suicidal or enraged the morning after, that kind of thing. Dude's not perfect though. He's our ghost."

Fascinated, she swallowed another bite and asked, "Ghost?"

"Disappears and we have no idea where the fuck he is. All of us on the team have lost Gray at one time or another. A knife-wielding psycho isn't as likely to take me down as Gray disappearing on my watch." He rubbed his chest. "That damn near gave me another heart attack."

She tried to keep a wince off her face at the mention of his heart attack. He'd been physically cleared to work on the security detail. "You look good. Strong and healthy." More than healthy. Unable to help it, she eyed his thick, muscular arms in his T-shirt. He'd worn shorts, revealing his powerful thighs and calves. She'd seen women eyeing Ethan as they walked to the Flying Bridge.

"You checking me out, sunshine?"

Ana lifted her chin. "Just making sure you haven't gotten fat without me around to motivate you." Ethan was as competitive as her. She missed trying to keep up with him on the bike or kicking his ass on rollerblades. She could beat him in the batting cages, too, but anything else he'd leave her in his dust and laugh. She'd loved that too. Ethan never held back in competition with her. Nor did he get pissed when he lost.

His mouth curved. "I'm doing double duty as a trainer for the band. I work out with them as a group and individually around my bodyguard duties. It keeps me in shape. And since four of them have some skills in martial arts, we spar. It's fun."

"You do all that?" She had to admit she was impressed.

"Yep. It's helped me to pay off my debts faster, and I like it." He stole another fry. "Now it's your turn. Tell me how it's going for you."

She set down the second half of her wrap. "You ordered fruit instead of fries, eat it." She reached her fork over and speared a juicy chunk of melon. "I told you I graduated and that Kat offered me a promotion. She expanded from her original San Diego bakery to open branches in San Francisco and Los Angeles, and I was in on all that. Developing and implementing marketing plans for each one is a challenge." Excitement bubbled just talking about it. "I travel more and more now. Plus we're working on a Sugar Dancer product line of bake-at-home products, so I've been meeting with reps of various retail stores, pitching the idea, talking about possible deals. I'm learning so much." She cut herself off. "Anyway, that's my life."

Ethan snagged yet another of her fries. "You love it."

"I do. It's gotten even crazier with Kat and Sloane's wedding only a month away." Her boss was marrying Sloane Michaels, the man who'd found Ethan living on the streets as a kid and took him in. While officially Sloane, a former UFC heavyweight champion, had done it as part of the Fighters to Mentors program, the reality was Sloane had finished raising Ethan and was more of a brother than mentor. She asked, "You're coming to the wedding, right?"

Ethan set his iced tea down. "Yes. But I'll probably be leaving soon after that."

"But isn't Savaged Illusions's tour done then?" It took everything she had not to cringe with embarrassment. "I wasn't hinting that we could go together or anything like that. You're close to Sloane and I know he wants you there, that's all I was thinking. I wasn't suggesting anything more." She got it, they weren't dating. Ana had learned an important lesson that night when Ethan walked out—she had no right to use sex as a way to make someone want to be with her.

"I didn't think that, and yes the tour will be over. But I have a shot at an apprenticeship with Chef Siena. You met her at the party last night, right?"

That gorgeous, funny woman? He'd be working with her? Ana's food suddenly tasted like dry sand, but she managed to nod.

"I haven't signed the contract yet, but it's a fantastic opportunity. I'd get to work in several of her restaurants, travel with her and appear on some of her shows."

"Oh, Ethan, that's wonderful." It really was, even if she had a pang at the thought of Ethan spending so much time with the beautiful chef. "Where did you meet her?"

"A big party at her restaurant in New York. I was there as security for the band, and that night the band had me sitting with them because they know I like to cook. Siena came out of the kitchen to meet the band, and we started talking. She showed me her kitchen, and one thing led to another."

Incredible. Even she'd never imagined such a huge opportunity for Ethan. "You're going to be a real chef someday." Unable to help herself, she added, "Do you think you'll ever come back to San Diego? Maybe open a restaurant? You know Sloane would invest in you."

He leaned in close to her. "I screwed up, Ana. I let down a hell of a lot of people who believed in me, spent money and time on me, who were invested in my success as an MMA fighter. It wasn't just Sloane, but all my trainers..." He trailed off, clenching his jaw so tight it bulged at the joint. "I'll pay off every goddamned cent I owe, and I'm not taking another penny from Sloane. There are others out there who deserve his help. I had my chance."

The blazing cold anger at himself ringing in his voice made the fine hairs on her arms prickle. It killed her that he couldn't see how amazing he was for the very fact that he owned his blunder and was trying to make amends. "It was a mistake."

"Don't do that. A mistake is choosing the chicken when you crave a hamburger. Injecting steroids on a concise schedule is a choice to cheat. Don't make excuses for what I did." He looked out to the Gulf, his eyes hard. Unforgiving.

Ana couldn't bear his self-recrimination. Yes, he had screwed up, but he'd paid the price. He'd cooperated with the police in every way, and he'd been working to pay off his debts. How could she not respect that?

Ana laid her hand over his fist clenched on the table. "What I know is that you made a bad choice, and when it blew up in your face, you could have been an asshole. Instead, you took complete responsibility down to working your ass off to pay Sloane back when we both know he didn't ask it of you." Kat had told Ana that, but Sloane was extremely proud of Ethan for doing it.

His brutal gaze softened. "You always see the good in people, stubborn girl." He rubbed his thumb over her skin.

Wrong. But Ana didn't want to get into old crap. "How long before you have to leave today?"

"Couple hours."

Smiling, she asked, "How do you feel about paddleboarding?"

Ethan hit her with an inquisitive stare, then seemed to make a decision and leaned in. "Does it involve you in a bikini?"

He'd never seen her in one, had he? "One way to find out. We'll stop by the resort shops and buy you a pair of boardshorts."

He leaned closer, his face inches from hers. "I want to see your bikini."

Her mouth dried. He was so close she could see the faint scar beneath his left cheekbone. His hand covered hers, his thumb stroking her wrist. His touch ignited the warm desire already pooling in her stomach.

This was her chance to experience Ethan. To indulge her fantasies of the one man she wanted.

Short term. This fantasy had an expiration date, and then she'd be alone again.

Ana was taunting him as they took their paddleboards around the Gulf. Her hair blew around her shoulders and face, and her skin glowed from the sun and lotion she'd spread all over to prevent a burn. Her sapphire-blue bikini top formed enticing triangles over her breasts, then bared more skin down her belly to her tiny boardshorts. Long, lithe legs braced apart to balance on the board as she paddled near the shore.

He really needed to think about something else besides how hot Ana was. "How's your stepmom?"

Ana smiled. "Linda's good. She turned forty this year. To celebrate, she and her sister are in Italy. It's a special trip for her. Honestly I think it's the first time she's truly enjoyed herself since my dad died."

Her dad's unexpected death had been hard on her. "How are you doing?"

She glanced over. "I miss him, but it's tougher on Linda. I had moved out, had my own life, and getting back to my routine helped. But Linda...well it took a while. Anyway, she's loving Italy." Her smile was sad. "Dad would be happy to see her living again."

She meant that. Cared that much about her stepmom. He'd asked her about their closeness after her dad's funeral. She'd said that Linda saved her when she was a teenager, but hadn't explained. He debated asking now, but let it go and instead said, "The band played a couple concerts in Italy. Beautiful country, and the food is incredible. Of course we went to Taste of Siena too. If your stepmother is in the Tuscany area, she should try it." He couldn't help but add, "I was invited to cook with Siena there."

"What was that like?"

"Amazing. She's bigger than life in the kitchen, a lot like you see on TV. Passionate, charismatic and very sensual. We both have the same love for food, for creating an experience that feeds more than just the stomach." How could he tell this girl what it was like to feel empty and unloved, and then discover that feeding yourself and others filled a void? "Creating a meal is an expression. Like fighting or sex. When a mother loves a child, she feeds him. When a man romances a woman, he feeds her. At every major celebration, food is central. Being in Italy, cooking in her kitchen, it felt...like home." He clamped his mouth shut. What was he doing going off on a tangent about his obsession with food or what it meant to him?

Her silence stretched before she turned and gave him a brittle smile. "I'm happy for you. You're going to be famous, and you're doing what you love."

Yet her strained smile didn't match her warm words. What was going on with her? "I'll stop talking about cooking. I'm boring you."

"No, don't stop." Her smile grew into a real one. "I want to hear it. I guess I'm a little jealous."

"Of what? You said you love your job."

She nodded. "It's silly, but some of my favorite memories are all the times you used to cook in my kitchen. Now you have these amazing experiences that trump those. In a few years, you won't even remember me at all. I'll be that girl claiming that I used to know you and you cooked in my kitchen and everyone will roll their eyes and beg me to stop talking about it."

The memories assaulted him. He'd show up with groceries, Ana would dig through the bags, excited to figure out what he was going to try making. She never shied away from tasting. Or if he forgot an ingredient, she'd run to the store, sometimes several stores.

And by the end of their meal, as they cleaned up, the scent of the food he'd cooked would cling to her skin. Marking her. Making him crave a taste of Ana, to kiss and lick her. Consume her. "I'm not going to forget that, or you. I had fantasies about you. I could smell my food on your skin, and it made me hungry for you."

Ana's eyes widened, the blazing sun brightening the brown to gold. "What kind of fantasies?"

He debated for a second. His fantasies were a tad rough. But that night when she'd kissed him and he'd taken control—okay lost control—she had responded. "I wanted to push you over the counter and hold you down. Ask you if you got off on teasing me."

Ana blinked, her mouth parting slightly with a huff.

Ethan waited, giving her a chance to see if she liked the idea. Her sexual experience had been fairly limited from what he could tell, maybe two intimate boyfriends before she and Ethan had become friends. She might not be comfortable with rougher sex. Except she'd said she wanted to let go and quit worrying. He could give that to her.

A challenge glittered in her eyes. "I was a good girl, remember?"

"What I remember is how goddamned sexy you were without even trying. And today? Look at you." He tracked his attention down her, taking in the tiny swimsuit over golden skin all the way to her toes with the blue polish. He lowered his head a fraction to lock stares with her. "You're not being good now, are you, Ana? You're purposely taunting me, getting me hard."

Her smug smile answered him.

He loved that she didn't hide it. Why should she? "Is that your fantasy? Driving me out of my mind?"

"Is it working?"

Ana deserved to have a fling as much as anyone else. And as long as it was with him, he'd make damn sure she was safe and satisfied. "You keep this up in the room when we're alone, and I'll show you what happens to bad girls who tease me."

"What?" Her fingers tightened on her paddle. "Tell me."

"Think hard, sunshine, because if I get you in that room and you taunt me, I'm pushing you up against a wall and those bottoms are coming down to your knees. If I touch your pussy and you're wet, I'm not waiting for permission. I'm going to bury my cock inside you. Hard, Ana. And you'll take it, all of it, and I'll make you come, over and over. Or maybe I won't...until you apologize for making me so goddamned hard for you day after day and burn for you every damned night." He heard the rough frustration in his voice, the truth of it. Even after he'd left, traveled the world and had plenty of women, it was Ana he wanted. Craved.

She shuddered.

Ethan searched her eyes, looking for fear. Nope, he didn't see it.

"What if I won't apologize? Maybe I'm not sorry."

He froze, going so still he could hear his own heart thumping in his ears. "Provoking me, sunshine? You don't want an orgasm?"

Her chin went up. "I know how to make myself come."

Christ. The very thought of her touching herself, showing him she didn't need him, inflamed his lust. But the defiance in her eyes intrigued him more. There was some need he couldn't define. Not yet.

"Hard to do if I have your hands pinned behind your back, fucking you slowly, keeping you right on the edge. Whispering in your ear to give in, just surrender and I'll let you come." He wanted that, forcing her to give him everything. The one girl he couldn't have, and he'd damn well have her.

Temporarily. That harsh reminder did nothing to

dampen his lust, it just added a layer of desperation to it.

"You still want to taunt me?" Jesus, what was he doing here? The more he let loose on the reins of his control with her, the more his desires for Ana surfaced.

Her eyes glowed with a blatant dare. "Two things."

"What?"

"I'm on birth control, but I want to use condoms. I'm not risking an accidental pregnancy."

He'd never take her bare. Ever. Ethan knew what he was—an ex-whore who didn't deserve to touch her. But since he was going down this path, he'd sure as hell protect her. "All of us in the band and security have routine blood tests. I'm clean. And I always use condoms, no exceptions."

"Oh, I—" The first sign of doubt clouded her expression. "I haven't had sex in a couple years."

Two years? And he thought he was going to take her hard? Hell no. He'd still give her the experience, but he was damned glad she'd told him that. It didn't change how much he wanted her; if anything it made him want her more. It just meant he was going to enjoy getting her ready. Driving her to the brink with his fingers...

Enough. He had to get them in the room before he was too hard to walk. "You said two things. We discussed birth control. What's the other thing?"

"Yes." She put her paddle into the water and pushed off, heading for the shore.

Confused, he called out, "Yes what?"

She glanced back over her shoulder, a sexy smirk riding her mouth. "I still want to taunt you."

Oh her ass was his now. Temporarily. He couldn't forget that. A few days, and he was gone and out of her life. He'd never risk his past rising up to hurt and humiliate her. Nor would he be able to bear that look of disgust toward him in Ana's eyes.

– Chapter 4 –

ANA SLIPPED INTO THE ROOM just ahead of Ethan and rushed past the two queen beds, through the dressing and bathroom area into the living space.

She grabbed a plastic container from the fridge, snatched up a fork, and hopped up on the counter by the small sink.

Her heart thumped, and chills broke out on her skin as Ethan strode into the room. He didn't look at her, but walked straight to the huge slider and pulled it open. He stayed there, hands hanging loose at his sides as he focused on something outside.

What was he thinking? If he dared to change his mind now, she might just push him off that railing outside the sliding door. Ana wasn't up for another rejection. But she had an idea of how to regain his attention. After popping open the plastic lid, she dug her fork into the rich pie that just happened to be Ethan's favorite.

He spun around. "What are you doing?"

"Eating." She shrugged, trying to appear casual. "I got hungry."

He stalked toward her. "Is that key lime pie?"

Ha, she had him now. "What, this?" She stuck the fork in, gathering a creamy piece along with a bit of whipped cream and crust, and held it up between them. "Why yes, it is. I always heard Florida has the best, so I thought I'd try it."

"Right now? While I was standing there at the window, trying to keep from ripping off your suit and fucking you blind, telling myself to slow down because you haven't had sex in a couple years and might need a little tenderness...you got hungry?"

Did he just growl that last part? The realization that she hadn't lost his attention, but rather he'd been struggling for some control, sent a wave of triumph through her. And affection that he'd thought he had to slow things because of her dry spell.

"Yep." She slid the small chunk into her mouth. It really was excellent pie.

His eyes heated to pure blue, like the center of a gas flame. He slapped his hands on the counter, bracketing her hips. "Are you going to share?"

"Nope." She scooped up another bite and got it halfway up, when he caught her wrist and tugged it to his mouth.

Damn he moved fast. Before she could recover, his lips closed over the forkful. A low sound of pleasure vibrated in his throat.

Ana couldn't tear her gaze from him as he slowly savored the morsel. Heat radiated from the pit of her belly. "That was mine."

He dipped his finger into the whipped topping and spread cool, sweet cream over her mouth. "And this is mine." He swiped his tongue over her lips, lapping the treat.

The warm, wet licks sucked the air from her lungs.

Ethan tangled his fingers in her hair, holding her

still as he cleaned off the whipped topping with an intensity that shivered through her. Not enough, it wasn't nearly enough. After dropping the pie on the counter, she sank her fingers into his thick hair and darted her tongue out to meet his.

Ethan groaned and deepened the kiss. Sliding his hand to her jaw, he tilted her head back and demanded she give him full access to her mouth. Wild need surged, and she couldn't get enough of his taste or the feel of his skin still hot from the sun.

She wrapped her arms around his neck, almost climbing up him.

His chest heaving, Ethan gripped her sides, pushing her back onto the counter. Breaking the kiss, he glared down at her. "No you don't. You're done teasing. I'm barely holding on to any restraint. We're doing this slow."

"I don't want slow." She wanted to just lose control and wipe out her ability to think or worry.

"Tough." He settled his hands on her bare thighs and skimmed his palms up. "I'll give you what you want if you tell me you're sorry for teasing and promise to be good."

The bastard was goading her. Paying her back. Given his massive hard-on, she knew she could push him over the edge of control. Reaching behind her back, she released her strap and yanked her top off.

Her freed breasts tingled from the cool air and Ethan's heated stare.

"Or, I could do this." She sank a finger into more of the whipped cream. She'd never done this kind of thing. But now? She had nothing to lose and could be as bad as she wanted. There were no emotional consequences. It didn't matter if he secretly thought she was asking for it. Hell she *was* begging for it.

And it was amazingly freeing.

Ana painted the dollop of cream over her nipple, making it pebble and her belly tighten.

Ethan grabbed her hand and closed his mouth over her finger to lick it clean. A second later he had both wrists pinned behind her hips, forcing her into an arch. "You're so going to be pay for that. I'm going to make you beg me to fuck you."

The helpless feel of his fingers locked around her wrists caused an excited rush straight to her core. She squirmed as her entire body pulsed with anticipation. She'd never been this needy before. But Ana loved it.

Ethan latched on to her nipple and sucked, his tongue lashing the sensitive tip.

Ana bowed at the sensation, struggling to free her hands. But it was useless, he was too strong. That thought made her clit swell and ache. She squeezed her thighs around him, desperate for relief.

After releasing her nipple, Ethan took her mouth, tangling their tongues in a frantic dance. His free hand clamped on her hip, dragging her to his hard cock and rocking against her.

"Let go." She wiggled, attempting to free her hands so she could touch him. Maybe push those boardshorts down and—

His dark chuckle sent shivers along her spine. "Nope. Not unless you really want me to release you, and we both know you don't." A smile curved his mouth, and his tone gentled. "You're beautiful, Ana. You always were, but like this? Hair wild, your skin glowing from the sun and desire. Nipples wet and puckered from my mouth..."

The tenderness in his voice breeched her defenses, causing something thick and scary to grip her throat.

His gaze on her was too much. Too intimate. She tried to twist out of his hold. "Ethan."

Catching her chin, he kissed her then said, "Are you going to be good? Let me take you slowly? Lay you down, pull off those bottoms and make you come? As many times as it takes, to get you ready for my cock?"

A voice in her head tried to tell her to say yes. Stop this wildness. But she didn't want to back down. She wanted to drive them both higher. "Not a chance. If you can't handle it, then you know where the door is."

His fingers tightened around her wrists. "Bad Ana." Kissing a path along her jaw, he said, "Ask me to fuck you." He slicked his tongue along the shell of her ear. "Nicely."

Who knew Ethan could be so evil? She liked it. But she wasn't surrendering that easily. Instead she sank her teeth into his shoulder.

When he jerked, she laughed. "I don't surrend—" Before she could finish, his mouth was on hers, fierce, demanding.

She dropped her head back as he licked down the curve of her neck.

A noise echoed in the room. With her heart slamming in her chest, her body humming and needy, Ana struggled to focus. "What's that?"

"My phone. I have to check it. I'm technically on duty." Letting go of her hands, he strode to the table, snatched up the device and read something. "I need to go back."

The cold air chilled her overheated skin. Ana slid off the counter, found her top and retied it. Disappointment weighed her down. "Okay." What else could she say? Work came first. Looking around the room, she realized she hadn't planned this very well anyway. Franci and Chelle could return at any time.

"Ana."

He stood right in front of her. She'd been so fixated on the thoughts, she hadn't heard him move. Steeling her spine, she got over her frustration and smiled. "Operation Kiss 2.0 is thwarted again. Some things just aren't meant to be."

"It doesn't have to be over." He leaned closer. "I'm not ready to call it quits. Come with me."

"With you? Where? To the venue?"

"Back to where I'm staying at Bayside Manor. Come to the show with me tonight. I'll get you VIP tickets again, and then after the show, we'll go back to the manor. Spend the night with me." He laid his hand on her cheek. "We'll have more privacy in my room there. And more time to explore this need of yours to be my bad Ana."

The enormity of the invitation left her spinning. He was giving her more than she'd even hoped for. They'd actually spend real time together.

But was this smart? What if she couldn't really handle having sex and sleeping with him?

Really? Ethan's giving you what you wanted, and now you're getting cold feet? What did she think would be better? Have sex, then him walk out? That wasn't what she wanted either. Yeah, she accepted that they weren't going to have a future romantically. But if she truly wanted to be bad with Ethan and make some memories for both of them, why not take this opportunity and enjoy it to the fullest?

She could do this, and more importantly, she wanted to. Ethan was making a sincere effort for her.

"I'd like that." The logistics of the plan took shape in her mind. "I need to tell Franci and Chelle where I am. Are you sure it's okay if I stay? Is it a hotel?"

"Private manor we rented. Let me check with Hank,

but I'm pretty sure Franci and Chelle can stay at the manor too. That way you won't be alone at the concert, and you'll have more fun with them around."

A million thoughts skidded through her head, but one stood out. "I'm not sure we can afford the cost. The tickets, the rooms at the manor...maybe we should just—"

"There's no cost. I can get you the tickets free, and the manor's already rented." He leaned down, brushing his mouth over hers. Raising his head, he said, "Say yes. The place is huge, right on the bay with a boat and watercrafts. There's a big home theater, a game room, walking trails, you guys will love it. You don't have to rush back here. We can have some fun."

The fact that he actually desired to spend time with her stirred something that had gone cold and sad the day she'd sat alone in her doctor's office, waiting to hear whether or not she was sick. For the first time in a while, Ana felt wanted.

But it was only temporary. She couldn't forget that as she had no intention of getting her heart broken.

Again.

She hadn't been sure what to bring, but finally she and Ethan were out the door and heading down in the elevator. Franci and Chelle had returned right after she texted them, and they'd all been running around the room, changing and packing. The two girls would drive the rental car to the manor once they were all set to go.

Ethan's voice cut in to her thoughts. "Is it always like that?"

She glanced over at him. "What?"

"That...chaos?"

Chuckling, she said, "Three women trying to pack

and get ready in one contained space? Yep, that's usually how it goes. I'm guessing you don't have any sisters?"

"Nope."

Ana peered at him as the elevator stopped and opened to a courtyard. "Do you have any siblings?" All he'd ever told her was that before Sloane found him, he'd run away from home, lived on the streets and sometimes did underground fighting to survive. But he'd shut her down if she asked anything else.

"No." He laid his hand on her back as they walked, hauling her suitcase behind him.

There he was, quiet Ethan. She could feel the second he pulled away from her. When he withdrew like that, it burned. Worse, she could sense the pain that he held onto with an iron fist. It tugged at her need to fix things.

Despite his hard jaw and straight-ahead stare, she asked softly, "What happened to—?"

"Ana!" a male voice called out.

Surprised and confused, she spotted a dark-haired man dressed in tan slacks and a polo shirt striding up to them. He shot a quick look at Ethan then settled his brown eyes on her.

It was so unexpected, it took Ana a second to place who he was. It clicked finally, and despite the slightly humid air, goose bumps rose on her arms. "Gregory? What are you doing here?" She barely knew him, and she really wanted to keep it that way.

A grin tilted his mouth. "I'm as surprised as you are. In fact I wasn't even sure it was you when I called out your name. I'm here on a business trip and staying at the Guy Harvey Outpost. What are you doing here?"

Business trip? And why was he practically bouncing

on his toes like a two-year-old waiting for a cupcake?

Because he was waiting for you.

Ana rubbed her arms, suddenly cold despite the blazing sun. What were the chances that the man she'd been trying to avoid for the last two weeks had shown up in another state the exact same time she did?

"You knew I was coming here. You were in the bakery the day I booked the flight." She remembered it because Gregory had overheard her on the phone and commented on her trip. *You can use the plane ride to Florida to read my book.*

Gregory waved a hand. "Oh, right, you're on vacation. Actually that's a lucky break then. You'll have time to discuss my mom's book and a contract to write your dad's biography. Why don't we meet for drinks and—?"

"Ana doesn't have time. She's with me."

She stiffened at Ethan's ice-cold voice. Shooting him a glare, she said, "Quiet." It was bad enough she hadn't handled things with Gregory as well as she should have. Okay, she'd been avoiding the problem. But she didn't need Ethan taking over. She'd fix it.

"Who are you?" Gregory asked.

"Her date."

Gregory eyed the suitcase, then shifted to Ethan. "Ana and I are friends, and we're working together on a project." He returned his focus to her. "You've read the book, right? And my proposal? We should get started right away on your dad's story. I know I can get a big publisher to pay attention to a story about Roger Kendall, the home run king."

Unbelievable. It was like Gregory had rewritten reality into a version he liked. Time for her to be absolutely clear. "We're not working together. I told you no, and I meant it. I'm not going to read the book

you wrote or hire you to write my dad's biography."
She didn't know how to be more specific than that.

He stopped bouncing. "But you said you would.
This is my big chance. Publishers wouldn't even read
my mom's biography, but they'll fight for your dad's.
This will get me in the door. You have to—"

"Stop." She'd had enough. "The answer is no. It's
not changing, and you need to leave me alone. Don't
email, call, text or wait for me in the bakery."
Frustrated, ticked and a little frightened that Gregory
had actually arranged to show up where she was on
vacation, she stomped away.

"Listen to her, or you're dealing with me," Ethan
added.

Ana struggled to calm down and think. She'd talked
to Gregory twice before he sent her his book through
email. That was the moment she'd realized that he'd
mistaken her casual chatter as something more. She'd
told him she wasn't interested and avoided him after
that. Ignoring him hadn't worked, so what should she
do next? Should she call her dad's lawyer that had
helped Ana and Linda settle his estate? Absolutely,
she'd do that today. What about notifying the police?
But Gregory hadn't made any threat, so...

"Who is that?"

Ethan's sharp question slowed her spinning
thoughts. "Gregory Yates. He calls himself a sports
biographer, but I think the only thing he's written is a
book on his mother, who was a professional tennis
player before he was born."

"So this guy's been bugging you, and you didn't say
anything? What the hell, Ana?"

Like she wasn't concerned enough? Yeah she'd
seen that Gregory continued to hang around the
bakery, trying to talk to her. But Ana had been

sidetracked and a tad more worried about the lump in her breast than a customer who didn't understand boundaries. She didn't need Ethan in her face about it now.

She walked faster, her irritation ramping up. "Why would I tell you? And what was that back there with you acting all caveman proprietary? *'She's my date. She's with me.'* You don't get to lay some claim on me when it's convenient but ignore me when I need..." Her eyes started to sting. *Shut up. Just shut up.* He hadn't even known, so she didn't get to lay that on him.

And jeez, get over it already. She'd had a little scare. Big fucking deal. People out there had real problems. Right now, she needed to focus on her more pressing issue of Gregory, not her self-pity because she'd faced a tiny ordeal alone.

"That wasn't a coincidence back there," Ethan nearly shouted back. "He was waiting for you to walk by. I saw him before he called out to you. He was watching, Ana. Are you hearing me?"

She'd already figured that out for herself, but he didn't give her a chance to answer.

"A man followed you from San Diego to Florida, and I'm supposed to stand there and let him believe you're unprotected? I don't think so. I need to figure out if he's dangerous. Hell, what am I saying, he fucking followed you. He's a stalker. Jesus, how did you get involved with him?"

"I didn't get *involved*. I talked to him in the bakery because he looked lonely. His mom died, my dad had died, and we talked about it. He told me he'd written a book. It was two conversations and suddenly he emails me a book and a proposal to write my dad's biography."

He pinched the bridge of his nose. "You gave him your email address?"

The aggravation in his voice snapped the last of her patience. "It's on my business card." She stopped walking, realizing they were already in the parking area. "I'm not explaining myself to you. I didn't do a damn thing I should have to defend, but even if I did, it's none of your business. Either you want a few days of fun, or we call it quits right now."

His hard face softened. "How about a two-for-one deal? A few days of sexy fun and a friend who's concerned. Because that shit that just happened with Gregory has stalker written all over it. The guy followed you on your vacation. Let that sink in. Followed you from California to Florida, checked into the hotel right next to you and hung around until he saw you."

A chill rippled down her spine. "It's creepy."

He wrapped an arm around her, pulling her against him. "Stay at the manor for a few days. He should get the message. And if he calls or texts, ignore him. Don't feed whatever delusion he has going on."

That was very sound advice. "All right. Thanks. I'll call my dad's lawyer once I'm settled in. He'll know the best way to handle this." Ignoring Gregory hadn't worked, so she had to get proactive. It sucked to deal with it on her vacation when she'd hoped to get away from responsibility for a week.

Ethan opened his mouth, but Ana cut him off, done with Gregory. "I'll take care of it. Up to now, he's been annoying, but he crossed a line today. I'll give everything to my lawyer and handle it. Gregory will soon learn I'm no one's victim."

Nope. She'd lived through that once, and when she'd asked for help from her mom, all she got back was accusations. Yeah, her dad and stepmom rescued her, but at a high cost to them, one she wasn't really able to pay back.

So now? Ana rescued herself.

Ethan glanced over at Ana in the passenger seat of the Jaguar convertible. With the top down, the wind blew her hair, and she was struggling to tame it into a ponytail.

A gust tore the band out of her hand.

As she reached into her purse, fishing out another one, Ana's laughter pealed out.

That sound went right to his dick. So much better than her earlier worry and the sudden harsh withdrawal from him when Gregory confronted her. Ethan had automatically stepped in, making it clear she was his to protect. He didn't care if this was temporary. Someone threatened Ana, they dealt with him. It was that simple, except to Ana. She'd shut him down hard. Yet she'd had no problem letting him touch, kiss and restrain her wrists. That thought unleashed another torrent of lust. He'd always been attracted to her, but this? Christ, she was hitting all his buttons, the ones he purposely ignored.

His fantasies about forced seduction weren't a bad thing, but he avoided the intimacy that kind of sex game would require. It'd take real trust for a woman to allow him to hold her down, force her to climax for him and then bury his cock in her, wringing more orgasms from her, proving she wanted him.

"Your knuckles are white."

Her soft voice dragged him out of his introspection, and he loosened his hold on the steering wheel. He was too worked up. When he'd gotten the text calling him into work, he'd had the urge to ignore it. Turn off his phone and focus on Ana. He couldn't walk away from her again, not like he had eleven months ago. When she'd agreed to come to the manor with him, it had been an instant relief to know they'd have more time together. But right now, he had to distract himself from thinking about getting her naked.

Casting around, he searched for another subject. "You don't wear your glasses anymore?"

"Nope, I got LASIK."

She'd been cute in her glasses, but he liked her either way. "So are you still living in the condo? Or did you use some of your inheritance to buy another place?"

She sighed. "I'm so tired of everyone thinking I'm suddenly rich. Everything went to Linda. It's her money, not mine. Why don't people get that?"

He'd assumed Ana had inherited at least a portion of her dad's estate. She was his daughter, after all. "Some people might resent their stepparent getting all the money. Does it bother you?"

"No. I wish he'd lived. That bothers me. But Linda was the love of his life and more of a mom to me than my biological mother. I knew what was in my dad's will. None of this is a surprise or feels wrong to me."

Ethan studied her in between watching the road. She tucked the flared skirt of her sundress—the same one she'd been wearing earlier—tighter beneath her thighs to keep the wind from catching it. A bit of sadness clung to her, the grief for her dad.

But she really didn't care about the money.

Something else nagged at him. "Who else is bugging you about the inheritance?"

Her face twisted. "After years of near silence, my mom's been calling and texting me."

He never quite understood what happened with her mom. He knew Ana'd lived with her until around fourteen, then went to live with her dad. "Your parents never married, right?"

"Nope. That part of my mom's plan failed. My dad wouldn't marry her when she got pregnant. So she went to plan B, soaking him for child support. He paid, getting only minimal visitation in the deal."

"You don't like your mom much, do you?" Something he understood all too well.

"She's a gold digger. She married another rich guy just before I turned fourteen and moved us to Washington, making it even harder for me to see my dad."

"Why's she contacting you now?"

"Because she thinks I'm suddenly wealthy. Her latest thing is pressuring me about going up there for her husband's fifty-fifth birthday party."

"You going?"

"No." She fisted her hand on the leather seat.

Hmm. "You don't like him?"

"I'm not getting within a hundred feet of him."

The hairs on the back of his neck rose. Ethan steered around a truck then turned to her. *I'm no one's victim.* She'd said that a few minutes ago in reference to Gregory, but had she been her stepfather's victim once? Rage simmered along his nerve endings. If that bastard had hurt her... "What did—?"

"I don't want to talk about my parents." She forcibly relaxed in her seat and raised an eyebrow at him. "Unless you want to tell me about yours?"

Hell no. He didn't ever want Ana to know about that. He shut up and drove.

– Chapter 5 –

"THIS IS BAYSIDE MANOR?" ANA blurted out in awe. The massive gates slid open, and they drove up a long, winding road through lush lands and passed a few buildings. "What are those?"

"Recording studio with offices, and three casitas are scattered around. This place is owned by a record label."

Wow. The scope of the life Ethan was living sank in. Finally they reached a huge, multistory, sand-colored mansion overlooking Tampa Bay. The building had curving lines that made her think of a gentle wave. "This beats the hell out of a hotel."

Inside the house was even more breathtaking, all done in whites, ocean blues and sea greens. "How big is this place?"

"Not sure. Big enough for ten bedroom suites."

She crossed the cool marble floor, barely noticing the pristine couches stacked with blue pillows, to the wall of sliding windows that had been opened, leading to an outdoor room complete with a kitchen, thick-cushioned couches and chairs, a pool, and beyond that the bay and dock.

Back inside the house, she eyed the spectacular gourmet kitchen boasting two sinks, double ovens and even a pot-filler faucet mounted over a six-burner stove.

"Ethan," a new voice said. "I saw you come in on the security cameras. I have the tickets for Ana and her friends set aside for tonight."

It only took Ana a second to recognize the man striding toward them as Hank from the VIP party last night

"Chelle and Franci are on their way." Ethan checked his watch. "Probably ten or fifteen minutes behind us."

"Sounds good." Hank smiled at her then returned his attention to Ethan. "Preshow meeting in an hour at the Hyatt. The threat called into the venue has been checked out. No validity, but they brought in bomb-sniffing dogs anyway. You and I are going over there for a final update."

Ethan nodded. "Let me get Ana settled, grab a shower, and I'll meet you at the hotel." He guided Ana across the great room to an elevator.

"Why are you meeting at the Hyatt?" She had too many things she was curious about.

"The rest of the security team, staff and road crew are staying there. We'll go over everything for tonight's show."

The elevator doors parted to reveal another beautiful foyer.

"We're this way." He led her down a hallway and opened a door.

Ana walked into a living room with a TV, couch and a two-sided desk. She headed into the bedroom, taking in the huge king-sized bed covered in a thick white comforter. Her stomach fluttered. Going to the French doors that opened to a balcony overlooking the bay, she thought about all the effort Ethan had gone to for her, even inviting her friends. He was giving her everything she'd once dreamed of.

Ethan settled his hands on her shoulders. "Second thoughts?"

"None." She turned to face him. "Thank you for all this. You've gone to a lot of trouble. You didn't have to do this."

Surprise softened his face. "I'm happy to. That last night in San Diego, I wanted to do something nice for you, but you hijacked my plans and turned it into the most amazing night of my life by giving me a chance to cook with Chef Zane."

Part of her rejoiced, and the other part wanted to flinch in embarrassment at her stupidity later when she'd kissed him. But at least he had some good memories of that night too. It made her happy to believe she'd helped him see he had options. Back then, Ethan had been, well, depressed. If she'd helped him to heal and move on, that was good. "You're doing so well. Kat had told me you're happy, but I'm glad I have a chance to see it for myself."

He fingered a lock of her hair. "You worried about me?"

Every day and night. "Nope, I forgot all about you. Kat would bring you up, and she's my boss, so I had to pretend to listen."

He smiled, and he tugged her against him. "I'm going to make damn sure you never forget me." He lowered his mouth to hers in a slow kiss. Tender. The word slid into her brain, and sparked a need to push away the vulnerability that came with it. She didn't need slow and tender, that was for people in love. She and Ethan were just old friends indulging in a fling. Wrapping her arms around him, she kissed Ethan back, capturing his tongue, and sucking.

Breaking the kiss, he caught her hair, his eyes intense. "When you fight me for control, I'll fight back. And I'll win."

The knot that had tightened after seeing Gregory loosened. She didn't have to hold back as much with Ethan as she did with everyone else. He was only interested in sex and fun. "Can't handle it?"

Moving fast, he spun her, wrapped an arm around her and pinned her back against his chest. "You don't learn, sunshine."

Ana squirmed, but he had her arms locked to her sides.

"Still want to tease me?"

Oh yeah. "Thought you had to go to work?"

He slid his hand up her thigh. "If I find you wet, baby, I'm going to take you right to the edge..." He kissed her ear.

Ana tilted her head, giving him access to the curve of her neck.

"...and leave you like that." He tunneled his fingers higher up her leg, his cock long and thick against her back.

The feel of him surrounding her fueled her lust. Part of her wanted to rip her panties off and beg him to touch her. But she wanted to prove she could make him more crazed.

Forcing a laugh, she said, "So? I told you, I know how to make myself come." Lowering her voice, she added, "Want me to describe it?"

"Fuck." His hot breath feathered over her neck, and his arm banded tighter. "Witch. You're going to plead for mercy." His fingers edged over her panties when her phone rang.

Ethan tugged his hand out and growled his frustration.

Ana couldn't believe this. "I hate technology right now." She snatched her purse off the mattress, fished out her phone and looked at the screen. "It's Chelle." Trying to calm the lust searing through her, she put the phone on speaker and struggled for a normal tone as she said, "Hi, Chelle."

"We're here at the gate. How do we get in?"

Ethan took out his phone. "I'll open the gate for you." He punched in some numbers.

Ana added, "I'll come downstairs. This place is awesome. See you in a bit." She hung up.

Ethan tugged her back into his arms. "After the concert, no more interruptions. The only thing that will stop me is you."

She shivered, liking this demanding side of him. "Do you see a stop sign on me anywhere?"

"I'll definitely do a thorough search tonight." He stepped back. "Go get your friends. I need to take a shower, get dressed and go over threat assessments. I might not be back for dinner. Will you guys be okay? The cook will make something. You can eat with the band or scrounge up what you like in the kitchen."

Ana cleared her brain of sex. He had a job to do, and he was serious about it. It hadn't escaped her notice that Ethan was part of the band's inner circle. That he could just bring her and two of her friends here said a lot.

"We'll be fine. Thanks." She headed for the door.

"Ana."

She looked back. Her mouth dried. He'd stripped off his shirt and untied his boardshorts.

"Sure you can find your way?" He slid them down. Slowly.

His cock popped out, fully erect, long, thick, the head nearly touching his stomach.

Dear God. Still clutching her phone, she took a step toward him. Ethan stood there, sunlight haloing him, hair spiky from the gulf water, wicked-ass grin on his face. Her nipples tightened, and air locked in her lungs. She'd never seen anyone so magnificent. So big...everywhere. Not perfect—he had scars that marked him as a man who'd survived things she couldn't even imagine.

But damn.

Finally she drew in a breath. "Uh..."

"Uh isn't an answer."

She forced her stare up to his face.

"You teased me by taking off your bikini top and doing naughty things with the whipped cream. Thought I'd even the score." He wrapped his hand around the base of his cock. "Is it working?"

She wanted to touch every inch of him. Heat flooded her body, making her wet. So wet. He was showing her a side of him that enticed her mercilessly. She gripped the doorway between the two rooms. Erotically torturing each other was a game she'd discovered she liked. Ana upped the ante with, "Did I mention the dare?"

His hand slicked up to the head of his penis. Down. "No, I don't think you did."

"Last week, Franci and Chelle decided to get Brazilian waxes. They dared me to do it too."

He stopped jacking his dick, but he didn't let go. "Did you?" The words came out harsh.

"You'll have to find out for yourself. Later." It took everything she had to turn and walk away.

His dark groan followed her.

Ana was still buzzing from the concert. She'd had as

much or more fun than last night. But now she was thrilled to be alone with Ethan while the others went out clubbing.

Ethan unlocked the door to their room and stepped aside for Ana to enter.

She uttered a soft gasp. The coffee table in their room had a silver bucket, champagne and two flutes flanked by a tray of intricately designed chocolates and a second tray with chocolate-dipped strawberries. The candies were exquisitely crafted—one tiny square had a delicate lavender butterfly on the top of it. Another was white chocolate with dark chocolate latticework.

"You did this?"

Ethan closed and locked the door. He walked past her and called out from the bedroom, "I stopped by a chocolatier when I was out today and ordered this for you. Staff put it in here, along with the champagne."

His thoughtfulness touched her. She chose a dark chocolate topped with a swirl of white and red. She bit into it... Oh God. Luscious chocolate with notes of amaretto and cherry gave it a decadence that had her closing her eyes to savor it.

"Good?"

Lifting her lids, she got an eyeful. Ethan had stripped off his clothes and was yanking on a pair of sweats. She assumed he'd wanted out of his work clothes.

"It's delicious. And romantic." As soon as the word left her mouth, she regretted it. This wasn't a romance.

He tugged the champagne out of the ice, wrapped it in a towel and opened it.

"You're pretty good at that." She indicated the champagne bottle he'd expertly uncorked. He'd developed a sheen of sophistication over the last few months, but that shouldn't really surprise her since he'd journeyed a lot of the world in that time.

After pouring out the golden liquid, he handed her a glass. "Practice. I've tried to learn as much as I can in our travels. This is an exclusive Krug champagne. I think you'll like it." He selected a strawberry coated in a white chocolate. He held the fruit out. "Open."

She parted her lips, the delicate shell giving way to sweet, tangy strawberry.

"Romance isn't my thing, but sharing things I enjoy with you is. That hasn't changed even if we're crossing the line from friends to lovers." Ethan brushed his thumb over her lip. "Watching you eat has always turned me on."

Her chest filled at the depth of his words. Not romantic? That was the most sensual thing anyone had ever said to her. "You realize I'm a sure thing, right?" She wasn't going to change her mind.

"I know. But I hurt you once, and I'm not doing it again. I don't mean sexually. You want it hard, I'll give you that. I mean when this is over in a few days or a week, you're going to know you were more than a girl I fucked then walked away and forgot about. Is that clear enough for you?"

The flutters turned into full-fledged wings beating in her belly. This was what she needed and why she came to him. But what killed her was the torment in his eyes, the belief that he really wasn't good enough for her.

You're not here to fix him, she reminded herself.

"Crystal clear. Your turn." She chose a dark chocolate berry and held it out to him.

He leaned forward, biting into the treat.

She took a sip of her champagne, enjoying the crisp bubbles with a hint of...hell, she didn't know. All she could think about was the man in front of her. He was what she wanted. Craved. The wine could be vinegar for all she cared. "Like the strawberry?"

He set his glass down and turned all his focus on her. "Good, but it's not you."

A buzz raced over her skin, and her nipples tightened. "You want to taste me?"

"Taste is too tame a word." Stepping closer to her, he slipped the flute from her fingers and set it aside. "I'm not tame, baby."

Something dangerous glinted in his eyes, like a wild arc of electricity that couldn't be captured, there and gone. It tugged deep inside her, igniting a need to chase it.

He framed her face in his hands. "You've taunted and teased me enough. You ready to behave?"

That question kicked her heart rate up. Going up on her toes, she kissed him, unleashing an aggressiveness that surprised her. Demanding access, she thrust into his mouth, appreciating the sweetness of the fruit she'd fed him.

It wasn't enough. She ran her hands over his shoulders and down his chest, eager to feel every dip and valley, to know him as no one else did. Her Ethan. *Hers.* Gliding her touch over the ridges of his abs, she relished the twitch of his muscles. She kept up the torment until her fingers brushed over the engorged head of his cock. Hot skin beaded with fluid.

Ana's pulse ramped up at the sight of his erection, so big and hard his cockhead had pushed out of the top of his sweats.

Unable to resist, she stroked the crown, spreading that bead of fluid and—

A hand clamped down on her wrist. "No."

Stabs of pleasure shot out from his hold on her arm. "My cock is off-limits until you show me." The growl in his tone stroked her internally, while his firm grip touched a secret yearning buried inside.

Ana tried to free her hand as a test. No give. He didn't hurt her, not even a twinge, just held her trapped. A wicked flash of heat snaked through her, tweaking her nipples and sparking a throb between her legs. How far could she push him? Raising her chin, she said, "Show you what?"

His mouth curved, and he tugged on her wrist, dragging her off balance. Before she could catch herself, Ethan snapped his arm around her waist and lifted her of her feet so they were face-to-face. "Ask me again. Do it."

The feel of him locking her against his powerful body had her panting in excitement. Why did it turn her on? Easy answer—she didn't have to hold back. "Show you what?"

His eyes darkened as his other hand wrapped in her hair, preventing her from moving. He leaned a fraction closer. "Your pussy. It's mine tonight, Ana. You're mine." He slanted his mouth over hers, kissing her with a torrid fierceness.

Ana slapped hands on his shoulders, unsure if she wanted to try to fight him or yank him closer. Fire spread until she rubbed against him, desperate to relieve the growing ache in her nipples. What was he doing to her?

Ana broke the kiss. "Put me down."

He did as she requested and stepped back. "More than you can handle?"

After tugging off her shirt, she tossed it aside. "You're a lot of talk. I'm more a girl of action." She undid her bra and slipped it down her arms. "See, I don't make all these dire threats then never follow through. *'I'm going to make you pay. Make you beg*,'" she mimicked him. "And yet here I am, still waiting."

His gaze traveled down her throat, fastening on her nipples. "Keep going. Find out what happens."

She undid her jeans, shimmied them down and stepped out, revealing her black lace string bikini panties.

For one heartbeat, his eyes flamed hot enough to make her belly tremble. This was what she craved, to be the center of that intense regard. Knowing that in this moment he truly wanted her fueled her courage.

She slid the panties down her thighs.

"Bare." He took a shuddering breath and moved in a blur, scooped her up in his arms and strode from one room to the other.

Startled, she asked, "What—?"

He dropped her on the soft bed, leaned over and kissed her, hard, his mouth no longer savoring hers, but owning. Tongue demanding. Once he conquered her mouth, he went to the spot on her neck just below her jaw that made her moan. He kept going, kissing and sucking her nipples until she writhed with madness, each pull of his lips arcing straight to her clit.

"Everything, Ana. Show me everything." Not giving her a chance to think or answer, he pushed her back and knelt on the floor. His large hands caught her knees and pried.

Ana instinctively fought, not from embarrassment, but need, an unsettling impulse to see how far he'd go if she resisted.

Ethan's eyes blazed a challenge. "No more warnings."

She firmed her muscles to provoke him.

In one fluid movement, he shoved his hands beneath her thighs, yanking her legs up and apart.

Her breath whooshed out of her at how easily he had her at his mercy.

He draped her limbs over his shoulders and pressed a hand to her abdomen, imprisoning her on the bed. Slowly, he lowered his attention to between her widespread legs. "Look at you, so bare, wet and pretty." He glided a finger through her folds. Shudders wracked her as he buried his face between her thighs, his tongue exploring while he eased a digit inside, stretching and pushing deeper.

It'd been so long, Ana couldn't fight the sudden buildup of clawing need. "Ethan, please!" With nothing else to hold on to, she clutched his hair. The tension mounted, her belly drawing tighter, all her muscles clenching. Sounds spilled out, and she arched her back.

He latched on to her throbbing bud.

Ana exploded, her climax slamming into her. Hot, wild pleasure gripped her.

When she regained her breath, Ethan loomed over her, his eyes wild, jaw clenched. Tendons stood out on his neck. "More, Ana. Can't stop." His naked shoulders bunched, the power in him tightly leashed. "Don't say no."

Say no? Her desperation matched his. Ana shoved his sweats down and wrapped her fingers around his cock. "Now. I want to feel you inside me." She guided him to her.

His cockhead pressed against her opening. Ana dug her fingers into his back.

He groaned and began to push in. "Damn, you're tight. And wet. Christ." His jaw bulged as he tunneled in another inch. Then two.

The stretch as he filled her, the soft burn of her flesh yielding, fired her nerves. She lifted her hips, trying to get more of him.

"Never felt this good, this— Oh fuck."

Ana froze at the snarl. "What?"

– Chapter 6 –

WHAT THE HELL WAS HE doing? He yanked out of Ana's sweet pussy and fought to get his breath. He'd never been so damned stupid before. He didn't deserve to touch her bare, to experience her wet heat gloving him with no barrier.

"Ethan?" The uncertainty quivering in Ana's voice spurred him into action.

"Condom." He shoved up, kicked off his sweats and grabbed the packet off the bedside table. After quickly sheathing his cock, he touched her mouth. "You tasted so good I lost my mind for a second."

Slow down. He lined up and began pushing in. Ana was small, tight and so hot, he shuddered. Sweat broke out over his flesh, and need clamped his muscles.

"Now. Hurry." She gripped his butt, showing him how badly she wanted him. "I need to feel all of you."

Inhaling her scent shoved him over the edge of control. He surged inside, going balls-deep. "Mine, Ana. Right now, tonight, you're mine."

She hadn't bought him like those other women and didn't need anything from him but this—letting go together. With him, only him. The thought of anyone else having her, even touching her, ignited a torch of possession.

Her gorgeous eyes turned fierce. "I always wanted to be yours."

Oh fuck. That shredded him. Ethan had never had anyone for his own. Ever. Fire seared his belly, while lust singed his balls. "Then give it to me. Come again."

He gazed down her hot little body, her stomach straining as she rose to meet every thrust. He could feel the slick walls of her pussy clenching around him in vivid need for more release. So damned gorgeous. Dropping to his elbows, he changed his angle, forcing his pelvis against her clit.

Her eyes widened. "It's too much. Help me."

Just like that, she gave herself over to him. He thrust again and again. He slid his hand down to her ass, tilting her hips, and Ana's eyes rolled back.

"Yes. God." She came apart, her walls gripping him in spasms.

His fingers dug into her skin, pinning her to the mattress while he pounded into her. His climax raced down his spine, driving him deeper into her, then exploded. He came so hard, the world blurred.

Except for Ana.

Ana jarred awake, startled by the feel of a huge, warm body behind her and an arm draped over her side. Ethan. Realizing he was there drained some of the tension from her nightmare.

"You okay? You were thrashing around in your sleep," Ethan said.

"Sorry." She blinked to clear the cobwebs from her brain. "What time is it?" The room had blackout drapes, so she couldn't tell. But they hadn't gone to sleep until after three.

"Eight. What were you dreaming about?"

She sank back against him. "My dad on the roof, then it turned into you. I kept yelling at you to get off, but you laughed and said you don't have to listen to me. I just knew something bad was going to happen. You started to slip, and I woke up."

He wrapped her snugly against him and kissed her hair. "Do you have that kind of dream about your dad often?"

She didn't need her psych classes to tell her she already dreaded Ethan leaving her again. "Hardly ever. Go back to sleep."

"Yeah, like that's going to happen when I have your naked ass pressed against my cock."

His voice slid down her back, warming her. "Well now—" She tried to turn, but he held her firm.

"Stay put."

Surprised, she craned her head around to see him in the soft gloom. "Why?"

"Because I like holding you. Not rushing. This isn't something I get to do."

She could just make out his eyes. But it was the tone of his voice that made her think a part of him longed for something—maybe a connection that went deeper than sex? "Wake up with women?"

"With you. I never wanted to wake up with another woman. Right now, you're mine."

Not just any woman, but her. How could she not feel special with him? He'd always made her feel like she mattered. The warm, contented feeling of his arms around her added to the sensation. The truth was she craved this comfort as much as she did the sex they'd shared.

"There's something I need to know," Ethan said.

"What?" She rarely hid anything from him. He just never asked a lot.

"Did your stepfather touch you?"

This time, the shiver that slid down her spine was anything but sexual. "No. And it's gross to talk about him while we're in bed." Or ever.

"I don't give a shit. We're talking about it. There's nothing you can tell me that will change how much I want you. But if he hurt you, I need to know."

"He didn't." Old anger simmered up. "I didn't give him a chance."

Ethan threaded their hands together by her belly. "What happened?"

"I was thirteen, almost fourteen when they married. I didn't like him much and just stayed out of his way. But he started watching me." This time she couldn't repress the quiver of distaste.

"I'm right here. No one is going to touch you but me." He tucked her closer.

The sensation of Ethan wrapping his huge, powerful body around hers made her feel safe. "He started *accidentally* walking in on me taking showers or while I was getting dressed. He'd come into my room, shut the door, and when I'd be outraged, he'd say, '*It's no big deal, we're family now.*'"

Would Ethan believe her or think she'd asked for it? And why wouldn't he? Hadn't Ana all but begged him to screw her? Sick anxiety ballooned in her chest, making it hard to breathe. Why had she told him?

"He's a predator. That's a form of grooming a victim."

The words came out harsh, but the fact that he understood eased her fear. "You believe me."

He pushed up on his elbow and stared down at her.

"I believe he tried it, and you refused to be his victim. I hope you kicked his balls into his throat."

His belief in her was so vivid, she blurted out the unvarnished truth. "I didn't fight. I felt trapped and scared, so I ran."

"Do you feel trapped now? The way I'm holding you?"

She didn't know how he could be this understanding. "I feel protected. Not trapped." It was so easy to talk to him she kept going. "One day he came home from work early when my mom was gone. He knew she was gone. I panicked and left. Went to my friend's house and called my dad."

"And?"

"He was traveling, and I couldn't reach him, so I called Linda instead. She told me to stay where I was until she got there. My cellphone started blowing up with calls from my stepdad and later my mom when she got back home. But I didn't answer. Linda flew to Washington and arrived at my friend's house. I told her everything. Then she took me home."

"With her?"

"No, back to my mom and Don's, where Linda confronted my mom. Don was out, supposedly looking for me. Anyway, my mom denied it and said I was trying to get attention."

"Bitch."

"Yeah." Ana knew exactly what her mom was. "Linda didn't back down. She believed me and told my mom that I was going home with her. Of course my mom said no."

"Child support."

"Yep, she still had four more years to collect. So Linda pulled out her phone, accessed her bank account, and said, "How much for Ana to go home with me? You'll relinquish custody and can have visitation in San Diego. But never with Don, or we'll make public accusations that he's a creep intending to molest a teenage girl. I'll destroy both your lives. That's the deal. How much? I'll make the transfer."

Ethan shifted slightly behind her. "That's why you love your stepmom so much. I always wondered how you formed that bond with her."

Ana would give Linda a kidney in a heartbeat. "I had no idea she'd even help me, but what she did—no hesitation. She left work that day, got on a plane and came to my rescue. So yeah, I love her, and I'll do anything for her."

"So why pay your mom? Why not just threaten to expose the bastard?"

"Because Linda and my dad didn't have custody or any legal standing. They could have fought, of course, but the system is slow, and there wasn't any real proof. It was my word against my stepdad's that he was coming on to me."

He squeezed her hand. "Got it. So how much?"

"Almost a million. Linda made the first payment that day but obviously couldn't move all of it in one transaction. But it was enough to get me out of there. The thing is, my dad had money, but not enough to toss away almost a million dollars." She turned her head back to see him. "Do you see why I didn't want his money when he died? He was my hero when I needed him—both he and Linda. Why would I want more?"

Ethan studied her for a beat. "Some would. But not you."

"I don't. I was happy with them. And I tried to be a daughter they'd be proud of." She'd worked so hard to be perfect, to never ask them or anyone for help again.

Deep down she'd feared that one day her dad and Linda would come to resent her, to think that maybe she'd been looking for attention as her mom said. Or...

She shut it down. Going over old stuff was a waste when she was here with Ethan for only a short time.

"Let's talk about something else." She lifted their joined hands, and a patch of rough skin on his palm stirred another memory. Tracing the scar with her thumb, she said, "Remember the time you tried to cook roast duck?" They'd almost kissed that night, but her smoke alarm had gone off, jarring them out of the moment.

He buried his face in her hair, chuckling. "I deserved to burn the fuck out of my hand that night. I was so close to kissing you, I didn't even smell the smoke or realize the bird was burning."

"It's funnier now than it was then." She didn't care about the duck or her oven, but she'd been devastated that they'd lost the moment. Then once he burned his hand trying to get the sizzling pan out, she'd been worried about Ethan and hated his pain. Ana had insisted on taking him to the emergency room. "It's a pretty deep scar." She traced it along his palm, wishing she'd stopped him from grabbing the pan without a potholder.

"Battle wound, but I can cook a duck now. My sour orange duck is exquisite."

She laughed, leaning back against him. "You really do still love cooking, don't you?"

He was quiet for a minute, then said, "I told you I lived on the streets before Sloane found me."

Her stomach clenched, hoping he'd tell her more. "Yeah."

"I was hungry a lot. I'd hang out by dumpsters in the back of restaurants sometimes. They'd give me, or any of us hanging around, food. But anytime they opened the door, I would catch the scent. It was the sweetest torture. These amazing smells of roasting meats, herbs, citrus. I became addicted to them. Once I had real access to food, I wanted to recreate those smells. Only this time, I could eat it."

It killed her to think of him like that. She had to swallow against the pain. Food held such power for him. When he cooked, it brought out the youth in him, a joy. But how had he ended up starving and so desperate? "Why, Ethan? Where was your family?"

His fingers tensed around hers. "No family. Just my mother."

Ana stilled, barely breathing. That was the most he'd ever told her, always shutting down if she asked how he ended up a runaway. "What happened? What made you take off by yourself?"

"I ran away. Leave it alone."

The bitter ice in his voice chilled her, a stark contrast to his warm body and the soft bed. "You demanded to know my ugly stories but won't share yours." Despite his being right there with her, loneliness closed in.

"Shit." He took his hand away, rolled off the bed and went to the window, shoving open the draperies.

Light flooded in around Ethan. He stood there naked, his huge shoulders flexed, muscles standing out along his back down to his tight, round ass and powerful legs.

And yet, for all his strength, a thick desolation surrounded him.

After throwing off the sheet, she crossed to him. Regret and shame pressed down on her. She was trying to force something from him he didn't want to give her. Ana edged up next to him and laid her hand on his back. "I won't ask anymore. It's okay."

He turned his head, his eyes seeking hers. "My past won't stay there. People know. I haven't really kept it a secret, I just never wanted it to touch you."

Her breath caught at the turmoil churning in his eyes. What haunted him so? "Why not me?"

"Because you're my one good thing. When you look at me, you don't see that I came from a cesspool. My mother was a high-class call girl who eventually lost her earning power. But she noticed women taking an interest in me."

Horror seeped into her blood. "How old were you?"

He turned away, looking out to the water. "Twelve."

Nausea hit her belly. "She didn't."

"Oh she did. She created a whole market. She'd rent me out as a boy toy. Soon I became really popular among the rich and bored. They fucking owned me for however long they booked me for. My mother didn't care what they did."

Ana'd had no idea...none. His mother forced him to have sex with other women? At twelve? "She should be in prison. Tell me she's in prison!" Fury ate at her.

"She's dead. Overdose a year or so after I ran away."

"Good."

"Doesn't matter if she's gone." Ethan stared out the window into the blindingly bright sun. "I'm still a whore just like her."

"You're not! You got out of it." Her heart pounded at the quiet agony in him. "Ethan, it was abuse and not your fault." Didn't he see that?

He turned then. "I ran. Then I got hungry, really fucking hungry. And guess what I did to eat? I tried underground fighting and roughly half the time got my ass beaten. Mostly because I couldn't control my fury at being so powerless. And those damned sex vultures loved it when I came slithering back, begging to let me be their little fuck toy." He rocked, as if trying to escape a memory. "I can still hear them. *'Once a whore, always a whore.'*"

His shoulders swelled, and color stained his face. His body vibrated with anger. A rage he'd controlled ruthlessly around her, and now she was seeing it. Seeing more of the real Ethan.

She didn't know what to say to him, how to help. Yet everything in her wanted to take the pain away. "It's not who you are now. Look at you, Ethan. You're protecting the most famous rock band in the universe and on your way to being a chef." Now she understood his drive, the need to gain power in a world that abused him when he'd been powerless. "You're the man I admire and want."

He stalked her to the wall. "It's exactly who I am. It always will be. It's why all I can offer you is to be your dirty fantasy for a few days." He smiled sadly. "Just like you've been my fantasy of what I wish I could have."

"You can." Didn't he get this?

He shook his head. "I won't do that, ever. People knew what my mother was. No other moms would let their kids play with me. When I was still in school and ran into a woman who'd bought me, she was horrified that I was in the same school as her two kids and told me to never talk them, ever. I shouldn't be there at all. That school was for decent folks, not trash."

"She paid for sex with a child and judged you?" Outrage exploded, making her head throb. "That bitch should be in prison, and a woman who loved you would stand by you. You're not trash, and there's nothing dirty about you."

"Wrong. I was born dirty. The kid of a whore and a man who paid her. I ran away to escape that, thinking I was better than her, and ended up selling my services just to eat. Don't you see? I repeated the pattern. Then later when I got a chance at becoming a MMA fighter, I cheated with steroids, making me a whole different kind of dirty."

Anger and self-disgust hardened his voice, and turmoil churned in his eyes. "I'm breaking the cycle, here and now. I'm going to make something of myself, something that's not about using and degrading people or taking shortcuts. Once I've redeemed myself, then if I run into someone who knows my past, it won't matter so much. I'll have proved I'm better than just a whore and cheater."

The irony was so bitter, she almost wanted to laugh. This was the very thing she loved about Ethan, he had the integrity to own his mistakes like using steroids and fix them. But that same integrity kept him from letting her close to his heart.

Or more likely, while he cared about Ana, he just didn't care enough. One day he might find a woman he loved enough to take the risk of finding out if she'd stand by him.

All Ana could do now was be his friend and support him. Touching his arm, she said, "You're going to make it as a kick-ass chef. And one day you'll see yourself as I do. A man I respect, care about and trust enough to ask him to help me be bad for a while."

He opened his mouth—

"Wait. If there's anything I can do to help, Ethan, all you have to do is call me. I meet a lot of people in the food industry in my job. I even see Chef Zane, who was very impressed with you. If you need connections or anything like that, call me. Keep in mind, I've gotten

Kat on baking shows and other opportunities. I'm pretty good at what I do." She added a smile. "No strings attached. I know our little sexcapade is a one-time thing."

Sexcapade—the word was so stupid and shallow, not even close to what Ana felt with Ethan.

Cupping her cheek, he tilted her face up. "There's my good girl, always trying to help."

Not good enough. No matter how hard she tried, she always seemed to end up alone. But that was her problem, not his. She'd be fine, she always was. "I'm not here to be good now."

"No you're not. Lucky for you, I'm excellent at being bad." Gathering her hands in his, he raised them over her head and kissed her. Once he had her breathless, he leaned back, studying her. "Tell me how you want to be bad. Specifically."

She had nothing to lose by revealing the truth. "I like making you work for it. And I love making you lose control."

His fingers twined with hers tightened. His cock brushed her belly, hot, long and thick. "You do that. Last night, when you showed me your bare pussy, all I could think about was I had to taste you." His voice dropped to a growl. "Then you fought me. Refused to open your legs. Teasing me."

The memory of the way he'd taken what he wanted made her excited. Wet. "You know that feeling when you and I used to race on roller blades or bikes? You wouldn't give in, and neither would I? We fought all the way to the finish line."

"Adrenaline rush." His eyes darkened, and his cock branded her belly. "Is that what you felt when I forced you to give me what I wanted, then made you like it?"

Need splashed so hard, she trembled. "Yes. When

you do that, I stop thinking and just feel. And part of me wants to go further."

Ethan pinned her hands firmer against the wall. "How far?"

"I don't know, but I want to find out."

Lowering his mouth, he kissed her again then picked her up and laid her on the bed. "We're both too raw for that right now. I'm going to be gentle with you. I need to show you that side of me, before I show you just how far and bad I can be—if it's what you really want."

"I do."

"Then give me this. Last night I told you that I need you to know you weren't a woman I'd fuck and forget. I need the same thing back from you—to know I'm more than just your dirty fantasy. Let me show you tenderness and pleasure, and then we'll explore any fantasies we both have."

Her stomach liquefied with desire and more. He'd been badly used and yet he cared enough to want to share with her a side of him he hadn't shown anyone else. She tugged Ethan into her arms.

And too damned much of her heart.

– Chapter 7 –

"HOLD ON," ETHAN SHOUTED, TAKING the watercraft into a tight turn that sprayed up a wave right at Franci and Simon. The lead guitarist of Savaged Illusions coughed out a mouthful of water, totally making Ethan's day. Bastard had already showered them twice.

Behind him, Ana's laughter pealed out. His cock jumped. He'd missed her competitiveness and the way she threw herself into everything. Having her body pressed against his back, arms wrapped snugly around him, wasn't a bad way to spend an afternoon.

The sound of an engine to his left jerked his attention from Ana and his dick. A second later a wall of water slammed into them.

"Ha! Payback!" Chelle shouted. Lynx sat behind her on the machine, laughing his ass off.

Ethan chased them down, the wind whipping around, water spraying, the guys trash-talking while the girls plotted shenanigans and revenge. He couldn't remember the last time he'd had so much fun.

Getting low on fuel, he gestured to the others that he was going back to the dock. Once there, he secured the craft and gave Ana a hand to help her up. He kept hold of her hand as they walked back toward the house.

He wanted to keep going, get her in their room, strip those bottoms off her and bury his cock in her.

Again.

Being with her, hearing her laugh, her hand in his made him feel clean. But he wasn't. He'd never outrun his past, and he refused to let that shame taint Ana. He'd done the right thing telling her. Now she'd understand why this couldn't last more than a week.

Ana dried off. "I'm going in to use the bathroom and check my phone."

Concerned, he asked, "Have you heard from Gregory?"

"No. Stop worrying, I told you my lawyer notified Gregory that any further contact with me must go through the law office. And security at the resort also talked to him. They took my concern seriously, and informed Gregory that if he bothered me again, he'd be removed and banned."

Although impressed that Ana wasn't messing around after that confrontation with Gregory, Ethan still worried. "He could escalate. Stalkers tend to get pissed when they can't get to their target."

"He can't reach me here. The whole place is gated and guarded."

True, which meant he had to keep her here with him. "Don't go back there. You guys can stay here until you need to go home."

She rolled her eyes. "I'll stay while we're having fun, but I'm not here to be a burden. If you and I call an end to this between us, I'll have security escort me, Franci and Chelle to our room, pack and we'll move hotels. I've got this handled."

She kept saying that, and it was getting on his nerves. Couldn't she just let him take care of her a little bit? Right. Like the time she was sick and told everyone it was just a sore throat? By the time he got to her condo to check on her, she'd been burning with fever and scared the fuck out of him. He'd been damned closed to calling nine-one-one. After he'd dragged her to urgent care, he'd spent that night on her couch, not giving a shit that she insisted she'd be fine.

Fine his ass.

But arguing wouldn't do anything but make her more stubborn. "I need to check the duck."

She shot him a grin. "You just had to prove your duck dominance, didn't you?"

Ethan lifted an eyebrow as they walked in the house together. "You dare to question my duck dominance? You'll be eating those words, sunshine, when you taste my culinary delight."

"I tasted one of your delights this morning."

The image of Ana kissing down his chest and stomach to lavish attention on his cock seared his brain. His blood heated, and his dick engorged with a throb. She'd taken her sweet time torturing him, learning what he liked... He had to stop thinking about it.

Yanking her off her feet and up against his body, he fisted her hair, careful not to hurt her. "Making me think about you sucking my cock was evil, little witch." He pressed his hard-on into her belly.

Challenge gleamed in her eyes. "Don't burn your duck."

"Right now, I don't care if the whole house catches on fire." Not when he held Ana. Sweet and sassy as hell, and so giving it made his chest ache. "You keep it up, I'm going to drag you to the nearest private space, rip those shorts off and make you come."

"Tell you what. If your duck is as good as you claim, then I'll let you have your way with me. Anything you want."

Raw lust lashed through him. After she'd told him this morning she liked the adrenaline rush of a little force, he'd been thinking about it. "Careful with those promises, baby. I used to daydream about you in the bakery. I'd ask you out, and you'd tell me no. There are customers and your boss around, so I have no choice, I leave."

"That's a daydream? I think I've had sneezes more interesting."

He tightened his hand in her hair. "That's not the interesting part."

"What is?"

"I come back later, when the shop is closed, and it's just you in there all alone. No one to save you. Then I dare you to tell me no again."

The skin across her cheeks warmed to a golden color, and challenge sparked in her stare. "Maybe I'll make promises and change my mind. Once you're all hot and ready, I'll say no."

A shudder went through him. What was it about her? Before Ana, sex had been a cold itch to scratch. Emotionless. He never treated a woman badly, ever. He made sure they both got what they wanted and walked away satisfied. With Ana, it was a hot, fiery ache. "Think you can stop me? You taunt me enough, and I'll take you and make you like it."

Ana caught a handful of his hair. "Maybe I'm looking for payback. Eleven months ago, you left me after telling me I was too good for you. But do you know what I felt? Huh? Not good enough. I'm tougher than you think, and I might just lock myself in a bathroom and tell you to go fuck yourself."

He vibrated with the impact of her honesty and courage. She was a powerful combination of sexy vulnerability that captured his attention and wouldn't let go. It also fueled his need to make her forget her pain and scream his name in pleasure. Ethan nearly shuddered beneath the power of his desire for her. Would it ever recede? Or just get stronger?

One thing he knew for sure, if she wanted this, he'd give it to her. "I'm going to get us one of the casitas to spend the night in. It's secluded enough no one will see or hear us, so you won't have to worry if you want to scream, or even run out the door." He leaned closer. "Later tonight, you'll go there first. Then I'm coming for you, sunshine." He lowered his head, holding her tighter in his arms. His cock surged against her, but what mattered was Ana. They could surrender to what they wanted...as long as they both wanted it. He set her down before he lost the last shred of his control. "It's up to you if you want to yell at me or surrender."

She flashed him her megawatt smile. "If you want me to be in that casita tonight, your duck better rock my world, Chef Sexy." She spun and hurried off, her ass swaying in her tiny excuse for boardshorts.

Witch. Yet as he headed into the kitchen, trying to will his cock into submission, Ethan grinned. Ana needed him to want her so badly that he took what he craved from her.

The girl was turning him into a sap, making him wish he could be good enough for her.

Everyone gathered around the big table, diving into dinner and chattering.

Ana took a bite of the duck nestled in a crepe. Her mouth sent up a *hold the phone* signal. Her taste buds danced with excitement. She barely swallowed before taking a second bite. The rich duck meat married to the bright citrus embedded in a savory crepe ranked high on her best-thing-she'd-ever-tasted scale.

On her right, Ethan leaned close to her ear. "How's the duck?"

Tingles raced down her body from his sexy whisper. Swallowing, she faced him. "It's not the worst I've ever had."

His mouth curved with blazing confidence. "No?"

He knew how good he was, damn it. "But it's definitely the best. You've proved your duck dominance." Just saying it made her shiver more. "You win the prize."

His gaze burned with hunger. "I have the casita. The key—"

His cellphone went off.

Ethan frowned, leaning back to drag the device out of his pocket. Surprise registered on his face. "Siena is at the front gate. I see her on the cameras."

"The chef?"

"Yeah. Hang on." He put the phone to his ear. "Siena, what's up?"

Ana resisted the urge to lean closer. She could hear a voice but not make out any words.

"I see. I'll let you in." He fiddled with the screen then set the phone down.

"What's going on?"

"She came to work on the cookbook." He shifted uncomfortably. "We had a loose arrangement to do some work while I'm here, but I had no idea she'd just show up."

Disappointment settled hard, but she realized he

96

was in a tricky position. "Thought you hadn't signed the contract yet?"

"I haven't. My lawyer's looking it over, and we've gone back and forth on a few issues. One sticking point is if I'm helping develop and refine recipes for the cookbook, then my name goes on it. So..."

"You're between a rock and a hard place." Oh she got it. If he wanted a guarantee of his name on the cookbook in the contract, he'd better damn well be ready to work when Siena called. She forced a smile. "I understand."

"I'll grab another place setting." Ethan got up and headed into the kitchen.

River shoved back a length of the long dark hair the band's bassist was known for. "He and Siena talked about it at the VIP party after you left. But I don't think he knew then that you'd be here."

Ana nodded. "Should we leave?"

"No," Lynx said. "Hang out here. It's not a big deal. I rented an indoor climbing facility tomorrow. You don't want to miss that. It has a trampoline room too."

Ethan laid out a new place setting just as a bell rang. "That's Siena. I'll let her in. You all keep eating."

Ana watched him walk away, a sinking sensation in her stomach.

Ethan returned with the beautiful blonde next to him. Ana hated the wave of insecurity that passed over her. She'd quickly showered, leaving her hair to air-dry and skipping makeup. She wore shorts and a cute top, while Siena had her long hair clipped over one shoulder in a sleek style, polished makeup and a gorgeous shirt paired with white pants.

Siena smiled. "I didn't realize I'd caught you at dinner."

"No problem." Ethan led her to a chair. Once she sat, he filled her wineglass.

"Ethan, did you cook this?" Siena asked. "Duck and crepes?"

He held up the serving plate for her. "Yep. I made it for Ana."

She flushed with pleasure.

"Really?" Siena smiled at her. "Do you cook, Ana?"

"Only enough to stay alive, and I can bake if I'm following a recipe." She couldn't resist adding, "Ethan made the duck tonight to prove to me he could. The first time he tried to cook duck at my condo, he nearly burned the place down."

The entire table laughed.

"It's funnier now than it was then. He burned his hand pretty bad."

"Ah. That explains the scar on your palm." Siena took a bite of the duck wrapped in the crepe.

Ana tried not to feel a twinge of jealousy. Of course Siena'd seen the scar, it was right there on Ethan's palm.

"The two of you have been friends for a long time. And now...?" She raised her eyebrows.

"Operation Kiss 2.0 is a success." Chelle lifted her glass and tapped Franci's.

"That's right. They're more than friends these days," Franci said. "If my law career and your graphics design business don't work out, we should opening a dating service, Chelle."

Ana wavered between embarrassment and exasperation. "I don't think Chef Siena—" she used the woman's title, trying to convey to her two friends that the woman was important to Ethan's career hopes, "—wants to hear about my and Ethan's friendship."

"Really?" Chelle ask. "Then I probably shouldn't

have tagged Ethan's Facebook page with the posts of the two of you kissing out on the dock today. My bad."

Ana knew exactly when that had happened. She'd raced him to the Jet Ski—first one there getting to drive—and he'd caught her on the docks. Swinging her up and twisting her in his arms, he'd kissed her, hard and long. "You didn't!"

"Oh she did," Ethan said.

Pivoting around to Ethan, she muttered, "Sorry. You deleted it right?" Ethan used his Facebook page to showcase his cooking.

"Nope." He rubbed her back and grinned. "You're the one who told my potential employer I burned my first attempt at cooking duck."

Crap. She had done that.

Siena's laughter rang out. "True. She's probably not who you want to put down as a reference."

Her embarrassment deepened. Before she could think of a way to redeem herself, Siena said, "This duck is very good." The woman leaned toward Ethan, touching his arm. "Tell me your recipe. What method did you use to render the fat? And your orange sauce, there's an extra tang to it. What is it?"

Ethan explained, and the two of them launched into a detailed discussion.

Ana picked at her food as everyone else around the table talked about the rock-climbing outing tomorrow. She tried to focus on the topic and not on Ethan and Siena huddled together talking. Finally dinner was over, and staff magically appeared to start clearing.

Siena rose. "I'm going to go get my notes and computer out of the car. Is there a place we can work? We'll get it all sorted tonight and plan a time to test the recipes."

Despite the staff going in and out, Ana stood,

scooping up her plate and walking into the kitchen. It was huge, with an industrial fridge, two ovens, wraparound counters and a big island, all overlooking the deck, pool and bay. The view did nothing to tame her disappointment over her and Ethan's cancelled plans.

"I'm sorry. I'm going to try to wrap it up soon. Just an hour or two, and I'll be all yours." Ethan stood so behind her, she could feel the heat of him spreading over her.

She turned. "Would it be better if I left? Franci, Chelle and I can go back to the Tradewinds and give you some space to work."

"Hell no. You're not going back there, remember? Not with Gregory around."

He was right, but that wasn't his problem. "We can find another place to stay." She couldn't bear the idea of being in the way.

Misery clouded his eyes. "Don't go." He leaned down, kissing her. "Please. I'll get away as soon as I can. We'll save our casita plans for another night, but we can go for a walk or hang out in the hot tub, even go down to the game room. Anything you want."

He was trying, and that meant a lot to her. "Okay. Chelle wants to check out the theater room. I'll watch movies with her and Franci."

Relief curved his mouth. "Perfect. There's a selection of prerelease movies in there. A fully stocked wet bar, candy counter and popcorn machine. I'll come find you when we're done here."

A naughty thought crossed her mind. "Any porn down there?"

Grabbing her waist, he pressed her against the counter. "What are you suggesting?"

"I haven't seen much porn. Maybe once you're done,

I'll throw my friends out, then you and I can research the racy movies. And if we get warm in there..."

He dropped his forehead against hers. "You're making me hot. And you know it."

"Okay here's my... Oh sorry." Siena walked into the kitchen, carrying a computer bag.

Feeling much better, Ana grinned. "Work fast." She strolled out with the sensation of Ethan's heated stare following her.

It was after midnight when Ethan finally broke away from Siena. They'd done some good work, but he got a real sense of how demanding she would be. Which wasn't bad—she was going to pay him well, and a lot of doors would open for him after a year as Chef Siena's assistant. He'd be legitimate. The stain of his past as a whore and a fuckup would lessen.

Right now, he just wanted Ana. He headed to the theater, anticipation quickening his pace. The wall sconces cast low light in the large room. Ethan walked down the aisle between the sets of oversized recliners and spotted her.

Sound asleep.

He couldn't help but grin. Ana lay curled on her side, one hand tucked beneath her cheek. An empty bottle of Merlot and boxes of candy—including Ana's favorite Milk Duds—told him the girls had had a little party.

He assumed Franci and Chelle had gone to bed.

But Ana had stayed, waiting for him. Regret stabbed him that he'd let her down. Leaning over, he scooped her up.

"Ethan? What are you doing?"

"Taking you to bed."

"But I waited."

More regret piled on. "I know, baby. I'm sorry, I got tied up."

She rested her head against his shoulder. "I can walk."

"I've got you." He didn't mind. Up in their room, he laid her down, stripped her to her panties and grabbed some ibuprofen and water. She didn't seem that drunk, but he didn't want her waking with a headache. Once she'd taken the tablets and drank most of the water, he turned off the lights and climbed into bed. Gathering her against him, he stroked her back.

She went completely limp. Asleep.

Despite his aching cock, warmth spread in him. He liked taking care of Ana, liked that she curved against his chest, soft and trusting.

For eleven long months, there'd been an empty place inside him. Then she showed up, and it was like someone turned on the lights. He called her sunshine for that reason. He'd been in a dark place when she swept into his life, bringing a ray of light and a thin strand of hope.

This time next week, he'd be alone again.

He tugged her tighter against him, not wanting to let go.

But he had to. One day, his story would come out. Professionally, he'd handle it. Hell, in the culture they lived in these days, he'd probably be more successful.

But personally? It would hurt Ana or any woman. The stain of his past would mark them in the eyes of the world.

He wouldn't let that happen. Especially not to Ana.

His one good thing.

Ana woke up alone and blinked the haze from her

brain. After sitting up, she glanced around and spotted a note.

Went running, back soon with croissants. Be naked.

Still lethargic from the wine and candy, which upon reflection was not an ideal pairing, she got out of bed and stumbled into the bathroom, where she brushed her teeth and took a shower. The multiple jets blasting her skin chased off her sluggishness. Feeling much better, Ana wrapped in a towel and went back in the room to look for clothes.

Her phone vibrated on the nightstand. Picking it up, she frowned at a text from Gregory.

Why is your lawyer threatening me? I don't understand, you and I are friends, and we're going to be business partners. Oh wait, it's that guy that was with you, isn't it? I bet he's jealous of our friendship, so you had to act like it was no big deal. Look, I don't care about him, but you know how important this is to me. Those agents and publishers won't take me seriously, but they will now! And don't worry, I'll give you credit in the book too. We just need to get this deal finalized ASAP. I'm emailing you another copy of the proposal for your dad's biography, and a simple contract. We'll meet to sign the agreement and talk about the book. Call me soon.

Her stomach knotted, and she had to sink down on the bed. How had she not realized that Gregory and reality weren't well acquainted? Her palms were slick as she checked her email server. A new one from Gregory with attachments.

"Ana."

She jumped at Ethan's voice. He filled the doorway between the bedroom and sitting room. His white T-shirt was flung over a shoulder, leaving him in only running shorts and shoes. She tracked down his sweat-sheened chest, over his ripped abs, then caught sight of the white pastry bag in his hand. "Oh hi."

"You didn't hear me come in the room." Setting the bag and shirt down, he dropped onto the bed next to her. "What's up?"

She showed him Gregory's text. "I'll forward it to my lawyer, but you heard me, I told him no."

His loose mood iced as he read the message. "He's delusional and dangerous. He was really fixated on you in the conversation at Tradewinds. We'll go to the police here and tell them you've asked this guy to stop contacting you. Then once you're back in San Diego, if he contacts you again, you have some groundwork to hopefully have him charged with stalking."

How did it get this far? "I thought I was being nice. I felt sorry for him." That was the only reason she'd talked to him, and now she had a stalker who'd followed her to Florida. She forwarded the messages from Gregory to her lawyer.

Ethan rubbed the bridge of his nose. "Let's eat, and I'll grab a shower, then we'll go to the police station. After that, we can enjoy the rest of the day."

Right. Enough of her problems. Getting to her feet, she shook off her mood. "I'll make some coffee."

Ethan caught her hand and tugged her onto his lap. "I want to help you solve this before you go home. I need you safe. You get that, right?"

Warmth chased out her worry. This was exactly what she'd needed—to just feel important to someone for a little while.

– Chapter 8 –

"AFTER WE GO TO THE police station, we can meet everyone at the rock-climbing gym if you want to," Ethan said.

Ana pushed the elevator button. They'd had croissants and coffee out on their little balcony and now were on their way down to the first floor to see what everyone else was up to. "It would be fun, unless you have a better offer?"

"If you want to go, we'll go. Or—" He cut off when the doors slid open.

"Or what?"

He tugged her inside and pressed her to the wall. "While they're all gone, we'll use one of the casitas."

Her heart jumped a beat. "Casita." The idea intoxicated her more than the wine she drank last night. "I want that. With you."

He sucked in a breath. "You're making me hard again. I swear I can't get enough of you." The doors slid open, he took her hand and they walked into the great room.

Ana couldn't wipe the grin off her face. She loved

that he wanted her, that she was exciting him as much as—

"There you are. We need to get going."

Ana stilled, her smile freezing. "Siena? When did you get here?"

"Good morning, Ana." The woman nodded at her. "I stayed in a casita last night. Didn't Ethan tell you?"

She blinked, turning to look at him.

Ethan ran a hand over his hair. "She said she wanted to work on the descriptions for the recipes and review what we wrote together yesterday, so I offered her a casita." Shifting his attention to Siena, he asked, "Go where?"

"I had this fabulous idea. The kitchen here is quite adequate, so why not test our recipes? Let's hurry, though. We need the absolute freshest produce and seafood. By the time everyone returns from rock climbing, we'll have several dishes ready, and they can test them for us."

Ana couldn't believe it. "Now?" She ignored Siena to concentration on Ethan. "I thought we had plans."

"We do," he assured her, and said to Siena, "Let's do this tomorrow. I didn't realize you were coming last night, but I made time. I promised to spend today with Ana. We have some important things we need to take care of."

The woman's face tightened slightly. "I only have a few weeks to get this cookbook finalized and in to the publisher. One of the recipes I want to test is yours. If you want your name on the book, we need to focus on it." She turned to Ana. "Wouldn't you agree?"

Ethan's hand stiffened in hers.

Ana could feel the tension bleeding off him from the implied demand in Siena's tone and comments.

With a pained expression, he said, "We could shift our plans to tonight."

Part of her wanted to say no, but she was being childish. "Sure."

"Wait, we need to make that report." Ethan eyed Siena. "I have to take Ana to—"

"No." She didn't want Siena knowing her business, nor did she need Ethan going with her. "I'll take care of it." Releasing his hand, she said, "I'll go find Franci and Chelle and have them come with me." She headed for the doors to the deck and stepped out into the balmy air.

Chelle sat on a padded lounge chair, her hand moving in graceful sweeps as she drew something in her sketchbook. "Where's Ethan?"

Dropping onto another lounge, Ana tried to swallow her disappointment. "Going shopping for the freshest produce and seafood."

Chelle's charcoal pencil stopped moving. "Is he making you a special dinner? That duck last night was good."

"No. He's cooking with Chef Pain in My Ass." Oh yeah, that didn't sound bitter at all.

"Seriously? I saw her skulking around the kitchen this morning. Thought she left last night?"

"Me too. We have a change of plans." She told Chelle about Gregory's text, that Ethan thought she should file a police report, and her lawyer had agreed when he texted her back.

Chelle shut her sketchbook. "I'll get ready, but back to Siena. Ethan didn't tell you that she spent the night?"

"No." This morning, Ana truly had felt like they were getting closer, then they'd come downstairs to reality.

Why hadn't Ethan told her Siena was staying at the manor?

A day later, Ana, Franci and Chelle explored the game room and got into a heated battle playing a virtual reality dance game until Franci won.

"Pay up, girls," Franci taunted as she held up her phone.

Sighing, Ana looked at Chelle. "We may have been a tad overconfident."

"You think?" Chelle turned back to the camera and held up her sign that read, *This is my Loser Face*, then made a sad face.

Ana did the same.

Franci laughed and took the picture. "Posting to Facebook now." Looking up, she gave them her sweetest smile. "I'm tagging you both, of course. I wouldn't leave you out."

Chelle tossed her sign and pulled out her phone.

"No deleting," Franci said. "That was in the bet."

"We deserve it for making a bet with a law student," Ana muttered as she got out her phone and accessed her page. When the picture appeared, she couldn't help her laugh. "God, we look pathetic." She headed to the big sitting area.

"Oh, dolphin watching."

Confused by the abrupt shift in topic, Ana looked up at Franci. "What?"

"I have it on my agenda on my phone. I forgot about it with all the excitement, but I'd like to go. How about this afternoon? It's not too expensive."

Ana was torn. "Let me talk to Ethan when he gets back."

"Humph." Chelle sat on the arm of the leather

couch. "That barracuda has her claws in Ethan—you'll be lucky to get him back in one piece. She's downright possessive."

Ana's stomach tensed. Siena was gorgeous, but even more importantly, she and Ethan shared the same passion—cooking.

"I have to agree with Chelle," Franci said. "You saw her at the wine tasting. She kept Ethan's attention focused on her."

Last night at dinner—which she almost hated to admit had been a spectacular array of Italian dishes Ethan and Siena had prepared—Chef Barracuda had announced that she'd arranged a private tasting with a wine broker to go over some pairings. Then she'd graciously invited Ana, Franci and Chelle along for the tasting. It'd been fun, but Siena had done exactly as her friends said, hovering over Ethan like a dog guarding its bone. They'd gotten home late, and Siena had insisted she and Ethan get all their notes together for the cookbook.

Ana'd ended up going to bed by herself.

This morning, Siena had snagged Ethan for a Skype meeting with their lawyers to work out the language of adding Ethan onto her cookbook.

Ana was really starting to hate that cookbook.

She stared at her phone when she noticed a new comment on the photo Franci had just posted. "Gregory."

"What?" Chelle said.

She shook her head in frustration. "He commented below the pic Franci just posted on our pages. 'Ana, as the daughter of a star athlete, you should know the three traits of a winner: Hard Work, Discipline and Ruthlessness. I outlined those in my mother's biography. She lived by those, and so do I. And now you will too. You'll see, you'll be much happier and productive, and I'll help you. Call me, we'll get the contract signed and start work.'" She shuddered, a sensation of being watched creeping up her back. "He's not giving up."

"Who's not?" Ethan strode into the massive game room.

"Gregory." One look at Ethan, and her crawling-skin sensation calmed. Ana stood and walked to him. "He commented on a picture on my Facebook. I should have unfriended him, but he never contacted me through Facebook or even liked my posts, so I didn't think about it." She held out her phone.

Ethan tensed as he read it, his eyes cold and pissed. "Where's that book he sent you?"

"I deleted it." Had that been a mistake? At the time, she thought he'd go away. And really, she'd had other things on her mind.

"Screenshot this, add it to your file. Have the police talked to him?"

"Yes, but he told them it's a misunderstanding, a coincidence that he's there at the resort at the same time as I am."

His eyes narrowed in concern. "Maybe it's time I go see him."

Ana laid a hand on his arm. "No. That'll only complicate things, and he could file some kind of harassment report. The police said no contact except through my lawyer for legal matters."

Anger flickered in his gaze. "What if he doesn't give up when you return to San Diego?"

It wouldn't be Ethan's problem, that's what. The emptiness loomed like a wave rising up, ready to consume her. *Get a grip, I'll figure it out.* "My lawyer is getting the request for a restraining order ready. He says the fact that I'm Roger Kendall's daughter will help with that." Before Ethan could form arguments, she went on, "But right now, I'm here. Franci, Chelle and I were talking about going dolphin watching." Ana wanted to spend time alone with Ethan, but she also didn't want to abandon her friends.

His jaw hardened. "I can't. Siena is insisting we go to her restaurant to tape some test videos to see how I do on camera."

"Well, that's a no then." She refused to look at her friends, not wanting to see their anger or pity.

"I came to ask you if you want to come. We'll have a late lunch or early dinner there."

"Just you, me and Siena?" Huh, good to know her sarcasm was in perfect working order.

Tense silence hung between them before he said, "I'll try to get her to leave us to eat alone."

He looked harried and tired, but enough was enough. "She won't. And I'm not going to be a third wheel." Again. Nor was she going to sit here and sulk. "Franci, Chelle and I are going dolphin watching. It's a couple hours' tour. Will that be enough time for you to get the video shoot done?"

His forehead creased. "Yes, and this should be it. I think Siena's leaving tonight." He pulled her in for a kiss. "I know this isn't ideal, but hang in there, I'll get rid of her soon."

Ana wasn't so sure about that.

Ana came downstairs freshly showered after their dolphin-watching expedition, and caught sight of Ethan in the great room. She stopped, absolutely stunned. He was dressed in a tailored suit that set off his shoulders while emphasizing his narrow waist and hips. He suddenly looked older, sophisticated.

The strain on his face melted into pleasure when he saw her. "Hey, did you see the dolphins?"

"Yep." But she wasn't interested in dolphins right now. "You look amazing." She'd never seen him dressed so sharply. He wore the suit with a naturalness that exuded power and confidence.

"We did some of the video test in chef whites and..." he glanced down, a wry twist to his lips, "...this."

"A formal suit? Is it new? Doesn't seem like something you'd have on hand as a bodyguard."

"Wrong. I often work close protection for formal events, and it's better if I blend in." He strode up to her. "Since Siena wanted formal, I figured this would work."

Oh it did. "You look awesome." Jealousy flickered. She wished she were dressed up and going out with him. "Maybe we should put that suit to good use. Go out to dinner?"

A real smile curved his mouth. "Anywhere you want. Even if they're booked up, I'll use Justice's name to get us a table. Have anything in mind?"

"Not really." A frown weighed down her face. "I don't think I brought anything dressy enough to—"

"Ethan." Siena walked in on stilettos, wearing a black dress and her hair done up in a lovely twist. "Oh hi, Ana." She turned to Ethan. "My lawyers have the revised draft of the contract. They've sent it to your lawyers, and we have a meeting at the law office in an hour." She glanced at her watch. "We need to get going soon before the rush hour traffic. Hopefully we can get it finalized and have that done."

Oh come on! Ana stared at Siena's oh-so-serious face, then Ethan's tight one. She already knew how this was going to play out because, hello, anyone else seeing the pattern here? She almost opened her mouth, but clamped it shut instead. If she forced a choice, she knew how that would end. She was the girl he was screwing for a few days, while Chef Schemes-A-Lot held the keys to his future.

"No," Ethan said. "First, I haven't talked to my lawyers or seen the revision. I'm not signing it without a thorough review."

"I would hope not," Siena responded. "But it's the exact changes we discussed. Your lawyers are reviewing it, and a representative from their Tampa office will be there. The others will join us via Skype. You can go over it yourself in the car. I'll drive."

"Second," Ethan ignored her and went on, "I've promised to take Ana out, and that's what I'm doing. She's put up with enough interruptions. I already told you that in the car."

Surprised pleasure that he was choosing to spend time with her soothed Ana's irritation.

Siena straightened, and iron determination radiated from her. "Business comes first. The publisher wants an answer from me about the names on the cover, and I can't give it to them until we have a signed contract."

Ethan turned to Ana, his jaw rigid. "I'll be back as soon as I can."

Disappointment crashed into her chest. "You're actually going."

His mouth flattened. "It's business."

Indeed. "All right." She headed toward the elevator. The tightness in her throat made her mad.

"Wait, Ana," Siena called.

The click of the woman's heels on the floor pounded in Ana's head. She had loved Siena on TV, really enjoyed her fiery personality and flare. Watching her show, it was like she cooked with her entire soul.

Much like Ethan.

Now Ana'd definitely soured on Chef Siena Draco.

"Ana, please."

Fine. She fought to get the bitterness and jealousy out of her expression as she turned. But one look at Siena and Ethan brought home a harsh reality. The two of them were wearing beautiful, sophisticated clothes, while Ana'd put on shorts and a tank after her shower, her hair scraped back into a simple ponytail.

Which one of the three of them didn't belong in this picture?

Siena touched Ana's arm, and the scent of jasmine washed over her. "Ethan told me in the car that he was devoting his whole evening to you. Believe it or not I feel bad about this, and I know I've monopolized Ethan. To make up for it, I've made reservations for two at Nadine's Steak and Seafood. It's right on the bay. The food is amazing. It's on me as a thank-you. The two of you will have the entire night to yourself, I promise. No more interfering. But I just need Ethan for another couple hours, including the drive time."

Startled by the kind sincerity in the offer, Ana tamped down her earlier frustration. "That's very generous of you."

"Not really. I want Ethan happy working for me. And you seem to be a big part of his happiness. Anyway, the reservations aren't until seven. There's plenty of time if you'd like to go shopping for a new dress or get your hair done, whatever you like." She flashed her charming TV smile. "Forgive me for my workaholic ways? And forgive Ethan too? I'm not really giving him a choice here."

Before Ana could answer, Siena faced Ethan.

"There? See, I'm not a total dictator. Now you can finish business without feeling torn and enjoy your evening. I'll wait in the car." She sailed out.

Ana stood there, still fighting the sting she didn't want to feel, hurt at always coming in behind another priority. Even her dad and stepmom put each other first, before Ana. Not in a cruel way, but the reality was there. However her baggage wasn't Ethan's fault. "Okay, well, I'll see you later."

He strode to her, pulling her into his arms. "I swear I'll get rid of her this time. We're going to have our night. Dinner out first." His eyes darkened. "But I'm paying for it. I'm not taking you out on my future boss's dime. And then we'll come back here to our own private casita. I'll be back here at six thirty on the dot to pick you up."

Relief soothed away the sting, and anticipation bubbled beneath her breastbone. But she wanted to make a point. "Don't let me down this time."

Ethan slid his hand down to wrap around her hip. His thumb dipped beneath her shirt to skate over bare skin. "I'll be here and all yours." He kissed her and left.

She desperately wanted to believe him, but Siena really did have her claws in him, and how could Ana fight that?

She couldn't.

Ethan refused to be bullied. "No. I own my recipes." The contract put his name on the cookbook as promised, but added a clause that Ethan couldn't prepare the recipe outside of Siena's restaurants or shows, unless he gave credit to Siena in perpetuity.

"Ethan," Siena said, her eyes flat. "You're getting exactly what you asked for, your name on the cover and credit for the recipes in the book. But I own them, that's how this works."

He leaned back in his chair. "Fine. Buy the rights from me or split the royalties on the book. My lawyers will draw up the contract." He'd expected hardball and silently thanked his mentor for teaching him how to play. Yeah, he risked the whole deal, but while he was willing to pretty much sell his soul for a year, he wouldn't give up his rights to his recipes. "You already have my agreement not to republish the recipes for profit for a term of seven years." That he deemed fair.

Two hours later, he won the battle, with the language hammered out. When he checked his watch, it was six fifteen.

Fuck. Ana. He'd sworn to be to be at the manor at six thirty to pick her up. No way could he make it now. He stood, grabbed his coat off the chair and looked at Siena. "I'm late, we need to leave."

She raised her eyebrows. "We're nearly finished. They'll hold your reservation. Text her, tell her to wait."

His patience snapped. Ana had waited, over and over. For two days, he'd put business and his ambitions first. Not completely unreasonable if she was just some girl he was screwing, but Ana was more. A woman who'd been there for him when his world went dark. Now he was stringing her along like some meaningless hookup.

On top of that, Siena was fucking with him, manipulating to get between him and Ana. He'd begun realizing it yesterday but had wanted to let it play out to see how far she'd go. Pretty far. That meant she saw Ana as a threat to Ethan signing the contract, and she was willing to fight dirty. But Ethan hadn't intended to let Ana down again tonight, and guilt stabbed him.

"I'm done now. You have my terms. Meet them or the deal is off." He yanked open the door.

"Ethan, you can't leave. We came together in my car. You don't have a ride."

He refused to answer and left. Once he made his way out to the front of the building, he called for an Uber, then dialed Ana.

She answered with, "Are you going to be late or canceling?"

Another guilt-blade dug in. He'd make it right. "I'm leaving now. An Uber is on the way to pick me up."

"Why an Uber?"

"Because I just walked out, and an Uber car is close by. Can you meet me at the restaurant?"

"You really walked out?"

"Yes. This is our night, Ana." Low panic burned in his guts, and his neck muscles ached with the fear that she was done and would leave.

"I'll meet you at the restaurant."

Relief untangled his biting tension. "Perfect, my ride should be here any minute."

"Okay, but if you need something to entertain yourself while waiting, check out my Facebook page." She hung up.

Ethan pulled the phone away from his ear and loaded her Facebook page. A stunning image formed of her dark blonde hair, straight and sleek around her face, long neck and shoulders bared in a shimmering metallic gold dress that molded to her body and exposed her legs down to killer heels.

The second picture showed her back bared to her waist except for the straps riding over her shoulders and meeting in a twist at the center. That pretty dress cupped her ass, ending with a tantalizing slit. Ana looked back over her shoulder with a sexy grin that made his cock twitch and thicken.

Jesus, he couldn't breathe. All his ambition coiled into a knot of need, low in his belly, for only one thing:

Ana.

– Chapter 9 –

ANA ARRIVED AT THE RESTAURANT before Ethan. The steak and seafood house had a huge wall of fish tanks with brightly colored creatures swimming lazily, creating a soothing atmosphere. Soft music played in the background, and white tablecloths with gleaming silver added to the ambiance. Ana settled into booth. She pulled out her phone.

Would Ethan show up, or would Chef-Cock-Block find a way to stop him?

Her answer arrived one minute later when Ethan strode toward her. He tugged off his suit jacket, the shirt clinging to his shoulders and arms as he tossed the garment on the opposite seat then slid into the booth next to her. His huge body took up three quarters of the seat, while his scent—warm and spicy—made her want to lean in to him.

Wrapping a hand around her nape, he tugged her to him. Heat simmered in his blue eyes. "Those pictures were hot, but you're more stunning in person."

Another first for her as she never posted sexy pictures. "You liked them?"

"So much that I've been walking around with an aching cock."

"Would you like to start with a cocktail or glass of wine?" Their server appeared tableside.

Ana repressed a laugh. Had the woman heard? She didn't look outraged if she had, so no harm done.

"They have an excellent Wagyu steak cooked on hot stones. Or did you have something else in mind?" Ethan dragged his thumb over her jaw, apparently unfazed. "Anything you want."

"The steak sounds good. Can they cook mine closer to medium?"

He gave the order, and once the waitress left, he said, "Tell me about dolphin watching earlier. I need to think about something else besides kissing you and how good you look in that dress."

Ana told him stories, showing him pictures of dolphins through the appetizer course. After a couple sips of the smooth Malbec, she got up the courage to say, "So, what happened in your meeting with the lawyers?"

He told her about the sneaky clause giving Siena ownership of his recipes.

"You stood your ground."

"On my rights? Hell yeah." He poured a bit more wine in her glass. "Then I looked at the time and realized how late it was."

"I thought you were cancelling."

His fingers clenched around his wineglass. "I was furious at myself. I got caught up in the fight and didn't watch the time. When Siena pulled her crap, she meant for me to let you down again. I was done."

Concern edged into her. "Will she rescind the offer?" Ana didn't intend to come between him and the job he wanted so badly.

His jaw tightened.

The server returned, bringing their stone-cooked steaks, the aroma wafting into the booth. "Is there anything else I can get you?"

"We're good, thank you," Ethan answered.

Ana stared at her meat sliced on a bed of greens, surrounded by baby potatoes and broccoli. It looked delicious, but Ethan's earlier silence left her uneasy.

"She overplayed her hand."

"Siena?"

He nodded. "The last two days, yeah. All the games to keep you and me apart. Obviously she saw you as a threat. Then the changes in the contract today trying to tie me to her indefinitely by owning my recipes. That tells me how important I am to her." Cold, brutal ambition hardened his voice and made his eyes flat, icy.

Ana leaned back. "How can I be a threat to you signing the contract? We're not even together. I mean not really. Not after this week."

He raised his eyebrows. "She doesn't know that. Once I sign, I'll be traveling all over with her, and most girlfriends would object to that."

Doubt crawled in, and she didn't like it. "Why does it feel like I'm a convenient pawn in your contract negotiations?" *Really?* She knew Ethan better than that. Okay he might use a situation to his advantage, but then, so would she when working to get deals for Sugar Dancer Bakery.

The chill in his gaze cracked as surprise and regret took over. "No. Jesus, Ana. It's a coincidence that you and Siena are at the manor at the same time. It just worked out this way and gave me an opportunity to see that she is serious about signing me." He frowned. "You knew this was my goal."

The words hit her like a reality slap. She didn't have any right to feel hurt or possessive. She was the one who'd approached him with this temporary fling proposition. If it came down to a choice between Ana or his job with Siena, his choice was clear.

"Forget business." Ethan stroked her face. "Right now I'm only interested in pleasure. Our pleasure." He cut a piece of her steak and held it out. "Try some meat."

Ana took a bite, consciously letting go of her insecurities to enjoy the food. Their time together was about sex and fun. The tense moment melted as they talked and ate. Finally she said, "I need to use the restroom."

Ethan slid out. "I'll pay the check."

Ana stood and hesitated. "I—"

He kissed her before she could speak. "I have it, Ana. I want to buy dinner. You're not a pawn to me. You're my lover and friend."

The sincerity riding his low voice reassured her. They were getting a second chance to redo the past and give each other good memories of their friendship.

You're such a liar. You're more in love with him now than a year ago.

Don't think about that, she told herself. *Not now.* Smiling, she said, "Thank you. It means a lot to me."

Rushing away, she remembered a small detail and glanced back at him. "I have the key to one of the casitas. Hank gave it to me."

It didn't take her long to locate the hallway that led to the ladies' room. Once she was finished, she paused in the small foyer that separated the bathroom from the door, and surveyed herself in the mirror.

Ana saw a deep fatigue in her eyes. She desperately wanted to just let go for a little while. She'd been holding on so tight, trying to make herself useful enough to the people she cared about so they wouldn't leave her.

Ethan *would* leave. There was a freedom in knowing that right up front. No matter what she did, he wasn't going to care enough to stay, so she could just be herself. For tonight, he was hers. Anticipation simmered in her belly.

Feeling a bit lighter, she stepped away from the mirror and opened the door.

A hand slammed into her chest and shoved her back.

Ana stumbled, her heels sliding on the slick floor. Shock confused her. What was happening? Struggling to catch her balance, she grabbed the wall dividing the bathroom area from the foyer. She jerked upright in time to see Gregory turning the lock on the door.

"What the hell are you doing?" She couldn't believe this.

He spun around, latched onto her arm and dragged her toward the three stalls. He kicked every door until he determined they were alone.

Ana regained her wits enough to yank on her arm. "Let go of me."

His fingers bit into her skin. "I thought you were so nice when I met you. And now I see you have a discipline problem."

Discipline? At six feet tall, Gregory was long and strong. He didn't have Ethan's muscle, but he was solid enough to overpower her. "You're hurting me."

He bounced the same way he had when she saw him at the resort. "I don't want to. When I first met you, I didn't think I'd have to. Your father's a star athlete, I thought you understood." He yanked open the handicapped stall door.

Oh hell no, she wasn't going in there. She clutched the edge of the stall.

Gregory reached his arm out to the right.

Ana started to turn to figure out what he was doing when a force hit the back of her hand. Oh God, pain exploded out. A scream tore from her throat.

His palm clapped over her mouth. "Shut up. There's no crying or screaming in discipline. You'll learn. Work comes first, not partying and goofing off. Work. Now sign the contract."

What contract? What is happening? She pressed her throbbing limb against her belly. It took her a second to figure it out—he'd slammed the stall door on her hand.

He dragged her to the counter. After releasing her mouth, he slapped a piece of paper down, then a pen. "Sign. Now."

Ana stared at the black ballpoint lying on a typewritten sheet of paper that had fold marks in it. In the mirror, she eyed the reflection of her injury. Carefully she moved the fingers. The pain had lessened but it still hurt.

Gregory jerked her arm. "Do it, pick up that pen."

She reached out with her good hand and fisted the pen. She had one chance—

A loud pounding sounded. "Ana?" Ethan called out. "You okay?"

Gregory grabbed her sore hand and tightened his fingers in a threat of more agony. "Say yes. Get rid of him."

Like hell. Ana bent her elbow, then snapped her fist down hard, jamming the pen into the lunatic's thigh. At the same time, she yanked her arm free and screamed, "No! Gregory's in here!"

Run. Don't look back. She hauled ass for the exit.

"Stay back. I'm coming in," Ethan yelled.

Ana skidded to a stop at the exact second the door flew open, banging against the wall.

Ethan stormed in, menace on his face. He didn't slow, but leapt into a flying tackle, hit Gregory and both of them slammed onto the tile floor.

Before Ana could blink, Gregory lay facedown. Ethan had one knee on the man's back and his arms pinned behind him. "You move, I'll rip your arm out of the socket."

"My leg. She stabbed me."

Ethan glanced at the bloody pen on the floor, then her. "You okay?"

She was still trying to take in how fast Ethan had moved. And the door... "You kicked it open. It was deadbolted."

"Look at me."

The gentle command pierced the wild pounding of her heart and buzzing in her ears. She focused on Ethan. Even in a half crouch over Gregory, strength exuded from him.

"Good. Now tell me if you're hurt. Where did he touch you?"

"My arm." She looked down at the angry red fingerprints. That would leave a bruise. "Slammed my hand in a stall door." She held up her arm and eyed it. No blood, but it was swelling and throbbed.

"Ana."

She blinked and returned her attention to Ethan. Shock, she wasn't focusing. "Sorry, I'm okay." She glanced at the doorway filling with people gawking at them.

A woman pushed through wearing a uniform. "Police. What's going on here?"

A cop already? "That was fast."

"I was in the area when a call came in. What happened?"

Ana filled in the police officer while the efficient woman checked Gregory for weapons and cuffed him.

"She stabbed me," Gregory whined. "Arrest her."

"You attacked me," Ana snapped.

Gregory glowered at her. "If you'd just read the book, you'd understand. Hard work, discipline and ruthlessness. I failed as a tennis player because I wasn't ruthless enough. Now I am. I won't fail, you'll see. You'll all see. When I write Roger Kendall's biography—"

"Not going to happen." Ana cut off his ranting. "Not now or ever."

Ethan wrapped his jacket around her shoulders, while keeping his scrutiny on Gregory. "How did you know where Ana would be?"

"It's on her Facebook. Bragging about her new dress for her date at Nadine's instead of working with me. I just had to wait for her to use the bathroom to get her alone."

Figured. Every time she tried to get a little bad, a little wicked, it bit her in the ass. "You need to get help, Gregory. And leave me alone."

Ethan drove the car through the quiet streets with Ana in the passenger seat. She hadn't said much, but she had to be tired. It had taken a while to give their statements, then the hospital trip to X-ray her hand. Thankfully it was only bruised, not broken. Ethan regulated his breathing, keeping a lock on his emotions. He'd take her to the casita—not for their fantasy game—but so she could rest without a bunch of questions.

She could have been hurt worse. The sound of her voice yelling, "*No! Gregory's in here!*" beat over and over in his head. What if he hadn't realized something was wrong in the bathroom?

As he turned onto the street leading to the mansion, more anger leaked through his control. He tapped his thumb on the steering wheel. Ana had no idea how close he'd been to ripping that bastard's arm out of his socket for the pleasure of hearing him scream.

She belonged to Ethan. She'd belonged to him since the day he'd seen her in the bakery. *Mine.* He knew damn well he couldn't have her. The stain of his past was a black mold that would grow and fester in the dark corners of her mind. It'd eat away at her feelings for him until she had nothing left but an ugly disgust.

"How'd you know something was wrong when I was in the bathroom?"

Her voice pulled him out of the pit, and he glanced over. She sat still, with the cold pack resting on the back of her hand.

After stopping at the wrought iron gate to the manor, Ethan used his phone to open it, then drove through. "A woman tried the door and found it locked. I heard her telling the manager." The hairs on the back of his neck had stood up as all his instincts went hot. "I knew something was wrong."

"Oh. Well, thank you. I'm glad you were there."

"What if I hadn't been? You weren't going to make it to the door. That bastard was right behind you when I got in there." That anyone would hurt her enraged him. "He's crazy and completely fixated on you."

"I'll handle it."

His control cracked. "Really? Because you've been doing an awesome job of it so far. Did you walk right by him in the restaurant and not even notice? He had to be by that bathroom watching for you. Oh and posting exactly where you were going to be at a specific time online? Genius. Fucking genius."

Silence spread between them, and Ethan clamped his mouth shut. He took the smaller road to the private casita then turned to Ana. She stared out the window at the two-story building in the glow of ground lights, her face pale, strained and remote.

He was an ass for yelling at her after she'd been accosted in the bathroom. He wasn't mad at her, he was worried and frustrated. "I'm sorry, that came out harsh. I have a lot going on. We're finalizing all the security on the last leg of the tour, I'm playing hardball on contract negotiations that can make or break my career." But what happened if Gregory got out of jail and returned to San Diego? Would he go after Ana? His aggravation at the situation built and shot out of his mouth. "The last thing I need is to worry about your safety."

"Then don't." Ana released her seat belt and faced him. "It's time to cut bait. This isn't working between us. I'll stay in the casita tonight, then fly home tomorrow and take care of myself. I always take care of myself."

Go home? She was leaving him? Panic closed in on his chest. Tonight, when he'd realized she was in trouble and a locked door stood between them, something had snapped in his brain. He'd have killed in a second to protect her. He didn't want to let her go. Struggling to breathe past the building pressure, the need to find a way to have her while proving himself to the whole damned world, he said, "Ana—"

She turned away from him and shoved open the door. "You'll be free to focus on the important stuff. Thank you again for dinner and helping me tonight. I told the restaurant to charge any damages, like the door, to me." She banged the car door and darted up the stone walkway.

Christ. He'd handled that like a champ. After ripping off his seat belt, he jetted out of the car and yelled, "Damn it, stop."

She spun around. "Go back to the house, Ethan. I'm done." She vanished inside, closing the door on him.

Who was the fucking genius now?

It took all his will to get in the car and drive away.

This was better for Ana. It didn't matter how much he loved her, it'd never work. His past would be exposed, people would gleefully dissect it, and Ana would feel the shame. He couldn't—

He hit the brakes so hard, the rear tires skidded, taking him into a spin. He gripped the steering wheel, hands sweaty, heart pounding and a crackling in his ears. His training kicked in, and he got the car under control.

Loved her? He'd always cared, but what did he know of love? Enough to love Ana, apparently.

After parking in front of the manor, he glanced in the rearview mirror and didn't like what he saw. A man who'd left the woman he loved alone, a woman who'd been hurt and terrorized tonight. But not before he'd made it clear that his job and his chance at an apprenticeship were more important than her.

No wonder she'd wanted to leave him. He was an asshole and clearly not good enough for her. He'd more than proved that this evening.

He should go in the house, tell her friends she needed them, and they'd go take care of her. If Gregory got out of jail, Ethan would do anything he had to in order to keep her safe, including break his contract with Savaged Illusions to protect her himself. Yeah, he'd be a fuck up professionally, but Ana would be safe.

That's what mattered.

Go inside. Yet, he couldn't. How much time had passed since he'd left Ana? Fifteen or twenty minutes?

The front door opened, and Chelle stormed down the steps toward their rental car when she spotted him. Pivoting, she jogged to the passenger side of Ethan's car, ripped open the door and dropped into the seat. "You're a jerk."

Ana must have called her friends, and Chelle had probably been on her way to the casita. "I know."

"I'm not done. I'm guessing Ana didn't tell you, or maybe she did but you're so busy with your new exciting life you don't care."

His guts clenched, and dread dug in. "Tell me what?"

The anger drained out of Chelle, leaving her pale. "Ana's fine. But for a couple weeks, she was scared to death that she had cancer. She went through it all alone." Chelle's eyes welled with tears. "We never knew. But the worst thing is she tried to tell us, but Franci and I were so busy dumping our problems on her, she never did. She went through finding a lump, the doctor's exam, mammogram, biopsy and getting the results by herself."

Jesus. He couldn't get his head around it. "I don't understand, how could she not tell anyone?"

Chelle looked away. "Because I'd gotten in way over my head with my graphic design business, and my boyfriend dumped me. Ana spent several nights working with me on QuickBooks so I could invoice customers correctly. She loaned me money to get me through. I'll pay her back. I swear it."

Guilt bore down on his chest, tightening it until he

could barely breathe. Ana had been fucking scared, and no one had been there. But it made sense why she hadn't realized how much Gregory was fixating on her in San Diego. She'd been distracted.

"And Franci's dad found out her mom was cheating. Ana helped him find a good lawyer and stood by Franci as she was torn in two by her loyalties to both parents. Plus Franci's been worried about paying for law school."

Ana hadn't said a word to him. Nothing. But she had told him repeatedly that she took care of herself. Obviously she had. Another thought hit him. What if the doctors had found something and she wasn't telling them? "Are you sure she's okay?"

"Yes. I only found out about the whole thing because I was at her condo and saw the biopsy report. She's clear, no cancer." She scrubbed the palm of one hand on her thigh. "She had no one. Ana refused to tell Linda about her cancer scare for fear she'd cancel her trip to Italy."

Ethan closed his eyes, knowing exactly why she hadn't told Linda. In Ana's mind, she owed her stepmom for helping her when she needed it. She wouldn't burden her again. God. He rubbed his chest.

"And tonight you told her she was too much trouble. All she asked was for you to make her feel alive and wanted for a little while. Like maybe she didn't have to be so damned perfect all the time. Ana's done this for so long, she doesn't know how to let someone else take over and help her anymore."

Her words slammed into him. All this time, Ana'd been telling him that. Asking him to let her have this fantasy with him where they could both lose control for a while. But he'd been too busy struggling with his demons and going after his big dream to really hear her. She'd been asking him for help, and he'd let her down.

Just like everyone else.

Then tonight, he'd been scared, worried, and lashed out at her, basically telling her she was a burden. No wonder she told him to leave.

"I'm going to her now, while Franci packs the rest of our things. We're getting her out of here, away from you, tonight."

Chelle's words snapped him out of his thoughts. "No, wait. Give me another chance. Please, just let me go to her now."

She lifted her head, eyes blazing. "Finally pull your head out of your ass?"

He blinked. A lot of people mistook Chelle's creative flightiness for stupidity. That was a mistake. The girl was smart and caring. She'd seen through Ethan when even he couldn't admit the truth.

"You either get real here and figure out you love her, or you let her go. What's it going to be?"

He'd known it the second Ana'd called out to him behind the locked bathroom door. He loved Ana, but would she give him another chance?

– Chapter 10 –

ANA SAT ON THE COUCH in the pretty casita with her knees pulled up to her chin, scanning the airline flights for tomorrow on her phone.

She couldn't concentrate.

"The last thing I need is to worry about your safety."

Ethan's voice rang in her head. Her throat ached more than the throb in her arm and hand. She wanted to hate him, but instead it just hurt. It was worse than when her mom refused to listen to her about her stepfather. She'd always known she was nothing more than a pawn to her mom.

But Ethan...deep down she'd thought he cared. Idiot. Hadn't he made it clear eleven months ago that she wasn't important enough to keep? Pressure built behind her eyes. She wished she could cry, just break down and let go for a while. Get some release from the swelling pressure inside her.

But she couldn't. Not anymore.

She hadn't cried since that day she left her mom's house. She'd tried hard to be good, not a moody or difficult teenager. No dramatics, no sobbing over boys or arguments. She'd trained herself not to break down. Yet the pressure inside kept growing. It freaked her out.

Like she was cracking inside where no one could see.

She glanced at the door.

She'd told Franci and Chelle what happened, but then insisted she was fine and would sleep here.

But wouldn't they check on her?

You told them you're fine. Why would they?

There was really something wrong with her. She didn't know how to ask for help anymore.

Except with Ethan. That twisted inside her, pain so deep she squeezed her eyes shut. *Help me.* The words had come out when he'd been deep inside her, driving her to pleasure so intense, it was the flip side of the pain she felt now.

And she'd had that same sensation of not being able to let go. But he'd helped her.

Later, she'd told him about her stepfather, and he'd believed her.

Then tonight he'd saved her.

And decided she was too much of a burden.

A click echoed in the room. Ana jerked her head up. What—?

The front door opened. She shot off the couch, her skin prickling. The terror drained once she recognized who was coming in. "Ethan." She didn't understand; he'd left, she'd heard the car drive away. "What are you doing in here? How?"

He lifted a key. "Master." He tossed it on the table and prowled toward her. "I'm sorry for being an ass tonight." He settled his hands on her face. "No job is as important as you are. The truth is, when I realized you were in trouble in the bathroom and that door was

locked, I freaked the hell out. Something in me broke—
I'd have killed anything that got between you and me."

"I don't..." She backed up, backing away from his
touch. This wasn't real. She'd learned that lesson twice
with him, and it had finally sunk in. Trapped between
the couch and coffee table, she had nowhere to go.
"Don't do this because you feel sorry for me. I'm fine."

His jaw flexed. "No, you're not. You were attacked
by a crazy bastard and I blamed you. Yelled at you for
not seeing him in the restaurant. Which, by the way, I
should beat my own ass for that. I'm trained to spot
trouble, and I didn't see him."

She didn't know what was happening here. "Okay.
But it doesn't change anything. I need to go home. I
know it was supposed to be just sex, but there's
something wrong with me." She didn't want to tell him
she was breaking inside. That she loved him so much it
hurt to breathe. She'd been a fool, lying to herself and
him. "I can't do this. I can't." She fisted her hands,
then winced at the pain in her left one.

Ethan caught her hand, gently caressing her
fingers. "Aside from your injuries from tonight, there's
not a goddamned thing wrong with you. You're the
bravest person I know. I'm the coward here, so afraid
to admit that I'm in love with you. I kept telling you I
was protecting you from my past, but it was me that
was afraid to take a risk. But you? I rejected and hurt
you once, and yet you tried again. That's brave."

She'd been desperate, not brave. Like she was too
close to the edge of a cliff and had no one to catch her
before she fell over.

Ethan went on, "You're my one good thing, and I
was too fucking stupid to hold on to it and fight to keep
you. Please, just stay a few more days, and I'll prove it
to you. I'll talk to Hank—"

His boss? "For what?"

"I'll leave the job and help you get through this ordeal with Gregory. You're going to have to fly back here for depositions and trial if it goes that far. Or if he gets off by some fluke, I'll be there to protect you."

"Ethan, no." He was upset and feeling responsible for her. "You're making promises you don't mean."

"Let me take care of you for a few days, will you give me that?"

Say no. Just go home. Stop this now. "I can't."

He looked down. "Okay. I'll make the arrangements for tomorrow afternoon. I'll fly with you on Savaged Illusions's jet, then meet with Sloane. He's going to make sure you're safe if Gregory is released and allowed to leave. Right now, let's get you to bed."

He was giving her up that easily? He really hadn't meant it. "I don't need you to stay."

"Too bad. I'll sleep on the couch, but I'm staying." Before she could form a protest, he got her up into the loft, helped her change, and tucked her into the soft sheets and thick comforter. Her head was spinning from the adrenaline crash, vulnerability and the pain pill he'd coaxed her into swallowing.

"I'll be right downstairs. No one can get in without going through me. Go to sleep." He kissed her forehead.

She didn't want to be alone. This was her last night with the man she loved. *You're not making sense. One moment you can't be near him anymore, and the next, you can't let him go.* But right now, he was all she had to hold on to. "Will you sleep with me?"

The harsh lines of his face softened. He climbed into bed and pulled her against him.

Ethan's warmth surrounded her as the drugs kicked in, pulling her under.

"I'm right here, I won't leave you. You're safe, Ana."

How was she going to face the rest of her life without him?

Ana stumbled down the stairs toward Ethan's voice. Who was he talking to?

"I want to meet with you alone first." Ethan stood in the small kitchenette, his shoulders tense as he held his cellphone to his ear.

Who did he want to meet with? *Siena?* Pain stabbed her chest and she hated herself for it. She knew how important the apprenticeship was to Ethan, yet she was jealous and wishing she could be that significant to him. But she wasn't. Her nose clogged and tears she couldn't shed burned her eyes. Her head ached.

Ana had been going to the coffeemaker, but she changed direction and went to the couch where she found her cellphone. After sitting, she unlocked the screen and stared in surprised. She had a dozen missed calls and texts.

"What's wrong?" Ethan moved up to sit on the coffee table directly in front of her. He grabbed a throw pillow, slid it beneath her injured hand, and arranged a cold pack over it.

She hadn't heard him finish his call. Had he just hung up? "My stepmom tried calling several times."

"News broke overnight that Roger Kendall's daughter was attacked in a restaurant bathroom. She probably heard and is worried. You need to call her."

"I will." She didn't want Linda upset.

"How's your hand?"

Beneath the ice and ace bandage, she gently flexed her fingers. "Little sore. It'll heal." She made herself look at him. *Tell him goodbye.* "It sounds like you have a meeting. I'll call Franci and Chelle—"

"Franci will be here in a few minutes," he cut her off. "I didn't want you alone while I'm gone."

Surprised, she blurted out, "You talked to them?"

"Chelle caught me last night as she was rushing to the car to get to you. I begged her to stay at the house and let me take care of you." He swallowed. "I'd hoped you'd change your mind and stay. Give me another chance."

Elation sprang up in her chest, but Ana shut it down. Hadn't she lied to herself enough? She was always going to come in second, and if she got in the way of his career, he'd resent her. It'd be like this week with Siena pulling him one way and Ana the other. And which way did he go each time? Siena. Ana wasn't enough. "I can't." Everything hurt at letting him go, but it'd be worse later when he finally realized he just didn't love her enough. "I'm sorry. I—"

"Don't apologize. You gave me two chances. I have to prove myself to you before you ever give me another."

Prove himself? She didn't know what he meant by that.

"We'll fly home this afternoon on the band jet. It's all arranged. I'll make sure you're safe in San Diego."

"Gregory's in jail here. You don't have to do that."

He smiled sadly, and leaned forward to push a strand of her hair back. "I want to. Please, Ana."

Then he'd be able to walk away with a clean conscience. Ana loved him because he was this man who would go to all this trouble. But then he'd go on and become Siena's apprentice. "Okay."

His eyes burned into hers. "One more thing. I'm sorry I wasn't there, that you didn't think you could call me and I would come. It doesn't matter what I say now, you won't be able to believe me."

"There for what?" She couldn't keep up.

"When you found the lump. For all of it. I can't believe you didn't tell anyone."

Stunned, she drew back. "You know?"

"Chelle told me last night right after she ripped me a new one for being a jerk."

Now it made sense. Why he was so upset and gentle last night. Between the attack and finding out she'd had the little tiny cancer concern, he'd felt sorry for her. *Tell him it's fine, that you're fine.* Instead she blurted out, "I almost called you. The night before the biopsy, I couldn't sleep and sat there holding the phone opened to your number." She slapped her good hand over her mouth. What was wrong with her? "I shouldn't have told you that," she whispered, her voice thick and raw. She was making him feel worse.

Ethan slid his hands beneath her and lifted her into his arms. "Ana." His chest rattled against her cheek as if he drew in a ragged breath. "I fucking hate that you were alone."

She had to fix this. Fisting his T-shirt, she raised her head. "I'm very lucky. Not everyone gets good results. But coming here to you, this was wrong, Ethan. I was using you, trying to heal something broken inside me. But you can't do that, only I can. And this—we're hurting each other. I know you care, but you have dreams." She loved him enough to want him to be happy. "Go after them and be successful. You have a meeting with Siena, right?"

Something fierce flickered in his gaze. "Yes."

She scooted off his lap and grabbed her phone and ice pack off the floor. "I'll call Linda and then get my stuff together."

Ethan rose and went to the small dining table. He scooped up his wallet, phone and keys then looked her. "I get why you can't trust me, why you didn't call me when you were scared. You were afraid I'd let you down."

She opened her mouth, but he went on.

"Hush. Give Linda a chance, Ana. She loves you. Think about how you'd feel if she kept something like a breast cancer scare or a stalker from you. What if she was in trouble and didn't tell you?"

The realization hit her dead center. "I'd be upset." She was beginning to realize just how much she'd hurt her friends too. She should have made them listen, and they would have. "I'll call Linda. And apologize to Franci and Chelle."

Relief eased a fraction of the tension in his jaw. "I'll be back."

She clenched her sore hand, the physical pain better than the ripping sensation in her heart. He was going after his dream exactly as she'd told him to. Every step he took toward the door cut deeper. She managed to say, "Good luck."

Ethan paused at the door, his gaze locking with hers. Then he nodded once and vanished.

Ana sank down on the couch and stared at the phone in her hand. Desperation clogged her throat. She needed help and reached out to the one person who'd rescued her in the past.

As soon as Linda answered, Ana spilled out everything from the moment she found the lump to now in a torrent of words.

"Honey, why didn't you tell me?" Linda asked. "I'd have cancelled my trip. Nothing is as important as you. You're my daughter."

She couldn't breathe past the swelling in her chest. "Linda. I—"

The door opened, spilling in Franci. Her friend's dark gaze swept over her, saw the phone in her hand and she waved an acknowledgement that Ana was on a call.

"Honey," Linda went on in her ear. "If you need me, I'll get on a plane and be there as quickly as I can."

Give Linda a chance. Half her instincts screamed to assure her stepmom that she was fine. But she wasn't. A man she barely knew attacked her, and Ethan...oh God...he'd told her loved her and she was terrified to believe him. A merciless fist in her chest squeezed her heart. "I don't know what I'm doing anymore. I love him too much."

"Ethan?"

"Yes. He said he loves me, but how can I know?" Unbearable agony swelled in her throat. "I really messed this whole thing up." The words clawed her throat. "He's feeling guilty or some responsibility and—"

"Wrong," Franci interrupted, striding up to stand over her.

Ana jerked her head up. "Linda, hold on, Franci's here and telling me something about Ethan." She faced her friend. "What do you mean?"

"He told me outside before he left—he's meeting with Chef Siena to turn down the apprenticeship."

"Wait, what?" Ana shot up to her feet, unable to believe it.

Franci touched her shoulder. "He's hoping it'll convince you he'd choose you over anything else. Even his shot at being a chef."

No. That's what Ethan had meant that he'd prove it to her. She'd refused to believe him when he told her he loved her, so he was giving up his dream for her. Sick agony pounded in her chest. She clutched the phone. The need to get to him gripped her. "Linda, I have to go save Ethan from a huge mistake."

"I heard. I love you honey. I'm booking a flight home, I'll call you later."

Ana stopped halfway up the stairs. "I love you too, Linda. I called you today because I needed my mom. That's you."

"Damn right, and don't ever forget it again."

That made her smile despite the urgency beating at her to get to Ethan. "I won't."

He'd let another woman come between him and Ana. That ended now. Siena might be able to give him a career, but Ana owned his heart. He didn't know if he could ever heal the damage he'd done to her trust. He'd finish the tour and pay off his debts, then go home to San Diego. He'd find a job and work hard to win Ana back no matter how long it took.

After parking, he headed into the building and straight to the conference room.

Siena waited by the window. "Why did you insist on this private meeting before signing the contract?" She strode to the table and slapped her hands down. "I'm not accustomed to demands from my apprentice. Before we do sign, you need to be clear, I expect you to be one hundred percent dedicated and passionate about the job. No distractions."

He stayed at the other end of the table. "Like Ana?"

"Exactly. I don't care if you're screwing random women, as long as they don't interfere with the job." Straightening up, she added, "You ever walk out of a meeting as you did last night, I'll fire you on the spot."

He narrowed his eyes and stayed silent. From a business perspective she had a point. But she'd been the one to arrange the reservations for him and Ana, making a big deal of reassuring Ana he'd be done by then. "You set it up to make me late or cancel."

"Damn right I did. From the second I met Ana at the party, I knew that girl was messing with your head. You have a huge future in front of you. The video tests showed you're amazing on camera. Your cooking is very good, though you need more experience, but that's something I can give you. You have a fresh, creative flair I'm looking for. But I won't accept you being distracted or telling me you have other commitments. For one year, you're mine. Choose—the girl or your career."

The ultimatum hung in the air. A week ago, cold dread would have filled him at the idea of failing to secure this apprenticeship. And this morning? "Thank you for the opportunity. I'm choosing—"

The door burst open. "Don't do it!"

Whipping around, he blinked in surprise. Ana stood there, her face flushed, hair wild, and wearing the dress from last night.

She rushed up to him and gripped his arm with her uninjured hand. "Don't. Franci told me what you're doing. Please, this chance means everything to you."

She'd come down here to stop him?

"Listen to her," Siena interrupted. "I'll open doors for you all over the world."

Yeah, she probably would. Ignoring Siena, he smiled down at Ana. His one good thing. "I don't want it. I want you."

"I'll wait. If you really want me, it's only a year. I'll wait."

The impact of her words sank in. Ethan was afraid to believe it. "You'll give me another chance?"

"Yes, but you don't have to give up this apprenticeship."

He pulled her against his side and turned to Siena. "I'm choosing Ana."

Ana stiffened. "Ethan, no!"

"Yes." He kissed her forehead. "I don't want to be away from you for another year. I'll get a job, I swear. I'll put in a call to Chef Zane to see if I can get a job as one of his line cooks. Or I can work for Sloane's security team, or another place. I'm going back to San Diego once the band's tour is over. I'm going to prove to you—"

"Touching." Siena cut him off. "But I wonder? Does Ana know all about you? I do. I had you investigated."

Ethan stilled, a vile taste slicking his tongue as a low drone of fury rumbled like distant thunder. He'd signed papers for a background check. Taking his arm from Ana, he faced the woman he'd once admired. "The steroid scandal is public knowledge."

"Yes it is. But this..." Siena picked up a dark gray folder, "...is not." She slid the folder across the table.

He raised an eyebrow, refusing to show a reaction, while his mind blared, *Once a whore, always a whore.* Were there pictures in there? The idea of Ana seeing him that way, a kid servicing women, exploded in his head, nearly making him vomit. All his instincts screamed to grab that folder and destroy it.

But he didn't move a muscle. To win Ana's trust, he had to give her his. And that meant trusting her with his worst moments and biggest regrets.

"Go ahead." Siena gestured to the file. "Show your girlfriend the investigator's report. You were a—"

"Child." Ana snatched up the folder, waving it in front of her as she stalked to Siena. "I know Ethan's truth. And I know this—if there's one picture, even one so-called testimony of someone who abused that boy, I'll have you arrested and charged with trafficking child pornography. I'll ruin you in ways you haven't even thought of. So tell me, Chef Siena, should I look in this folder?"

Siena's eyes rounded, and she stepped back. "Are you threatening me?"

Ana smiled. "Consider it an ironclad guarantee. You can't imagine the misery I'll rain down on you if you release this stuff. And I won't stop there. I'll rip your world apart until I find who took any pictures or told any stories of child abuse. Those women were all adults hiring a child. I'll destroy them too."

Ethan couldn't tear his gaze from Ana. She all but stole the words from his mouth, but coming from her? Defending him? It was a thing of beauty and filled his throat with so much love, he grabbed the back of the chair to keep upright.

"It's just a report," Siena blurted out. "No...no pictures. I—"

"Ethan, check." Ana held out the folder to him. "Let's see if we have the chef dragged out of here in cuffs today or not."

She didn't want to look for herself? He took the folder and flipped through the three pages. "No pictures. Only rumors and bullshit." He couldn't even be relieved, there was no room with so much love and amazement filling every one of his cells. It finally hit him—his past was just that, his past.

But Ana was his future.

"We'll take that copy as insurance." Ana turned from her stare down with Siena and walked out.

Ethan faced Siena. "You want to come after me, bring it. But you try to fuck with Ana in any way, I'll destroy you before she gets to you." He strode out and caught up with Ana in the parking lot.

She had her uninjured hand pressed against the side of the car, leaning over, panting.

He set his hand on her sweaty back. "You okay?"

She looked up, her eyes fierce. "I almost killed her. I could actually visualize myself doing it—leaping over that table, grabbing her throat and slamming her head onto the table. I was so mad. You were a child, and she tried to use that to hurt you. I hate her."

He kept rubbing her back. Her reaction wasn't surprising given her past. Ana had run, but she never got to face down her abuser. Today she'd faced down a woman that represented the ones who'd abused Ethan. "I've never seen anyone as amazing as you were in there."

Sucking in another breath, she stood up and touched his chest. "What about you? I'm so sorry. I know that was your worst nightmare."

The concern in her eyes reached into his heart. "I thought it would be. But seeing you go all Rambo on her ass, standing there defending me, no one's done that." How did he tell her what that meant? "For the first time in my life, I didn't feel dirty."

"I'll defend you. Every time."

He believed her. "I have to ask you something though. You handed the folder to me. Why didn't you look for yourself?"

"I don't need to. You told me what happened, and I didn't know what was in there. If there were pictures, why would I need to see those?"

This was what love felt like—this clean acceptance. He'd never known how freeing it was. He stared into the eyes of the woman who'd stood up for him. "I'm in love with you, Ana. You're my brave, beautiful and bad girl. If you need more time, I'll wait. I'll spend years proving myself to you if that's what it takes. I love you too much to give up."

Her eyes filled with tears. "I don't cry. I never cry. I can't—"

"Yes you can." He pulled her against him, stroking her hair. He didn't care that they were out in a public parking lot and people might see or hear. Ana was his, and she'd been too perfect and alone for too damned long. "You're mine now, sunshine. Let go, baby. You can always let go with me."

He held her close, the gift of Ana's love and trust seeping in to heal his heart. Once he was nothing more than a commodity to women, but to Ana?

He was the man she loved enough to defend, fight with, surrender to and trust with her most vulnerable moments.

Once Ana had been his one good thing, but now? She was his everything.

– Chapter 11 –

One Month Later:

"ARE YOU REALLY OKAY WITH the plea deal?"

Ana shifted in the passenger seat of the car to look at Ethan. She'd returned to Florida to meet with the District Attorney's office regarding the case against Gregory. Refusing to let her handle this alone, Ethan had flown in first, picked her up from the airport and went with her to the meeting where they'd learned the DA was offering a plea deal to Gregory for probation and mandatory treatment to be served in California. "I'm glad it's over, so yeah. Gregory's family lives in Los Angeles. He'll be settling there, and that's three hours away from us, depending on traffic."

Us. Ethan had been on the road for the last few weeks, but she flew out for long weekends with him. Next week he'd be coming home for good.

"How about you? Are you excited to start working for Chef Zane at Stilts?" Zane had offered Ethan a position as his apprentice. It would be long hours and hard work, but Ana was delighted for him.

"I can't wait. I like this job, and it's taught me a lot. But cooking is what I love." He took her hand. "Not as much as I love you, though."

She knew that. True to his word, Ethan had flown home to San Diego with her after her vacation ended last month, stayed a couple nights until Linda got home from Italy and demanded Ana stay with her a few nights. Turns out the two of them had anticipated Ana would have some nightmares in reaction to her attack, and they were right. Franci and Chelle were there too, along with Kat and Sloane.

She opened her mouth to tell him how much she loved him when he pulled up to a gate. "Bayside Manor? But I made reservations at the Marriott."

"I cancelled them and changed our plans."

"But..." Why was she surprised? Ethan had powerful friends. He just so rarely used them, and when he did, well it was almost always for her.

Ethan guided the car through the gates. "No one else is here at the manor, no staff or security, just us for the night." He turned off the main road that led to the house.

Ana recognized where they were headed and her heart started to thump. Her pulse jumped. "We're going to the casita."

"Yep. I made you a promise of capturing you, holding you down and taking you so hard you'd never again doubt who you belong to. I didn't make good on it, and that's unacceptable. I don't break my promises to you, ever. So I hijacked your cute little romantic night of dinner and sex for this, Operation Savaged Surrender."

Ana took off her seat belt, went up on her knees and braced a hand on his shoulder. "You did this for me?"

"For us." His blue eyes burned with intense love,

filling Ana. "When I promise you something, it will happen. You can count on that."

She realized that now. "Why Savaged Surrender?"

His mouth tilted up. "Because we're giving in to our savage sides and surrendering to each other. Totally surrendering, even me. What's the one thing you've been asking me for?"

Hot excitement shuddered between her legs. "Bare. I want your cock inside me without a condom." In the beginning, she'd wanted a condom in addition to her birth control as another layer of protection. In the last month, Ethan had shown her a love that was about true trust. If her birth control failed, the two of them would handle it together. But it went deeper for Ethan—taking her bare, especially in forced seduction, meant she accepted all of him, including his past.

"When I catch you tonight, you're mine. You're going to get all of me, sunshine, right down to my unsheathed cock."

His trust wrenched her heart and ignited her desire. Both of them were letting go on the deepest, most intimate levels. Ethan had feared his past while Ana had feared her inner bad girl. Tonight, they would truly surrender the last of their fears to an all-consuming love. Ana took his face in her hands. "I'll run and fight. You so sure you can catch and tame me?"

One of his hands curled around her hip. "I'll always catch you, but I never want to tame you. I love you exactly as you are."

Had anyone ever loved her this way? Before they lost themselves in this moment, she wanted to tell him how she felt. "For years, I got it in my head that people would leave me if I was bad."

Ethan closed his eyes for a second, then opened

them with so much love it floored her. "You're not bad, sunshine."

"But I'm human. I just didn't realize people would love me even if I wasn't perfect. You gave me that. You showed me that I could relax and be myself, and you'd still love me."

"Every damned day." His fingers glided over her cheek in a reassuring touch, but one that sank into with her the knowledge that this was what love felt like. Safe and free to be herself.

"You're the strongest man I know. You survived a life I can't even bear to think about to become the man who is my friend and lover." She kissed him and added, "I love you."

"I love you too. So much." His jaw hardened, and a wicked gleam flashed in his eyes. "You have five seconds. Run."

A sense of freedom and joy exploded through her, propelling her out the car door and running full bore. It didn't matter how tonight played out.

She'd already won because she had Ethan.

~ The End ~

Dear Readers,

Thank you so much for taking a chance on Savaged Surrender. I appreciate that you are choosing to spend your precious time with the characters and world I created. I'm truly grateful and honored.

This long novella is special to me because it links two of my series, The Plus One Chronicles and my upcoming Savaged Illusions Series. The hero and heroine of this book, Ethan and Ana, first appeared in The Plus One Chronicles Series as beloved secondary characters. After many reader requests, Ethan and Ana now get their own story in Savaged Surrender, and at the same time, give you a small taste of my forthcoming Savaged Illusions Series about a sexy rock band. I'll be releasing the first book in that series, Savaged Dreams, very soon.

I hope you enjoyed Savaged Surrender!
~Jen

Other Books by Jennifer Lyon

THE PLUS ONE CHRONICLES TRILOGY

The Proposition (Book #1)
Possession (Book #2)
Obsession (Book #3)
The Plus One Chronicles Boxed Set

THE WING SLAYER HUNTER SERIES

Blood Magic (Book #1)
Soul Magic (Book #2)
Night Magic (Book #3)
Sinful Magic (Book #4)
Forbidden Magic (Book #4.5 a novella)
Caged Magic (Book #5)

Writing as Jennifer Apodaca

ONCE A MARINE SERIES

The Baby Bargain (Book #1)
Her Temporary Hero (Book #2)
Exposing The Heiress (Book #3)

About the Author

Jennifer Lyon is the pseudonym for USA Today Bestselling Author Jennifer Apodaca. Jen lives in Southern California where she continually plots ways to convince her husband that they should get a dog. After all, they met at the dog pound, fell in love, married and had three wonderful sons. So far, however, she has failed in her doggy endeavor. She consoles herself by pouring her passion into writing books. To date, Jen has published more than twenty books and novellas, won numerous awards and had her books translated into multiple languages, but she still hasn't come up with a way to persuade her husband that they need a dog.

Jen loves connecting with fans. Visit her website at www.jenniferlyonbooks.com or follow her at https://www.facebook.com/jenniferlyonbooks.